MU
IN
FARMHOUSE

An addictive crime mystery full of twists

ROY LEWIS

Arnold Landon Mysteries Book 3

Originally published as
A Trout in the Milk

JOFFE
BOOKS

Revised edition 2021
Joffe Books, London
www.joffebooks.com

First published in Great Britain in 1986
as *A Trout in the Milk*

ISBN: 978-1-78931-824-1

Some circumstantial evidence is very strong,
as when you find a trout in the milk.

Henry David Thoreau,
Journal 11

CHAPTER ONE

1

'Arnold,' the Senior Planning Officer intoned, 'we have a problem.'

The Senior Planning Officer was never precise in these situations, Arnold knew. What he really meant was that *Arnold* had a problem. He waited, as the Senior Planning Officer belched gently and considered the difficulty.

They were standing in the corridor by the coffee-vending machine, a monstrosity which had been installed just three months ago and which was already the subject of litigation, having attacked one of the cleaning ladies attending to it. The authority defence was that it had leaned on her head, bruising it: the lady in question claimed it had leaped at her, and thrown her to the ground, pinning her down by its weight. She was consequently claiming for inhibition of sexual enjoyment. Her muscular husband reminded her of her ordeal by machine, and she could no longer enthuse over the sexual act. The Senior Planning Officer seemed unabashed by these events and visited the machine regularly, idling before it as though daring it to leap on him from its unsteady plinth. Perhaps he had problems with an overenthusiastic wife. The only complaints he had voiced to Arnold to date concerned her cooking.

The Senior Planning Officer returned the plastic cup to the shelf beside the machine and beckoned Arnold towards his office. 'Mr Wilson and Mr Livingstone will be joining us soon. Shall we go in?'

Arnold nodded and followed the Senior Planning Officer. His room was quite different from Arnold's. Its desk was broad, modern and highly polished. The carpeting, a deep, royal blue in colour, reached the walls, except under the window where no one would notice. There were always two sharpened pencils on the desk set and Annigoni's portrait of the Queen — a print torn, Arnold suspected, from an old newspaper colour supplement and discreetly framed — gazed serenely out over Morpeth, towards the distant sea, from the office wall. Arnold envied the Senior Planning Officer his office but knew, resignedly, he could never aspire to such magnificence: he was underqualified, inexperienced, and in the Senior Planning Officer's view, peculiarly subject to scandalous involvements with the police.

Publicity, in the Senior Planning Officer's eyes, was a Bad Thing.

'The problem?' Arnold inquired, sitting down gingerly on the edge of a chair as the Senior Planning Officer settled down behind his desk.

'Willington,' the Senior Planning Officer grunted. 'The Hall itself. And of course, its owner, Patrick Willington.'

'I'm afraid I'm not conversant . . .'

The Senior Planning Officer fixed him with a stern glance designed to wither. Arnold tried not to wither. Disappointed, the Senior Planning Officer scowled and said, 'From time to time there emerges what may only be described as a trial for this planning office. I'm not talking about the infernal objectors to road widening schemes, the professional troublemakers who turn up at inquiries and disrupt proceedings. No, I'm describing the kind of person who constantly makes planning applications that either have no chance of success, or are so complex as to cause us untold hours of work, only to have them withdrawn at the last moment.'

'Mr Willington?'

'Precisely.' The Senior Planning Officer frowned. 'The file is on the table over there. Pick it up when you leave at the end of the meeting. Included among those papers are all the applications that Mr Willington has made over the last fifteen years. There were a number before that; before my time.' He belched lightly, caressing his stomach with a soothing hand. 'Some of them caused us real problems. A hopper, for instance which was on wheels but could not be moved about the yard. Did that constitute a "building" under the acts?'

'Why couldn't it move?' Arnold asked.

'The weight of the hopper,' the Senior Planning Officer replied, 'had caused the wheels to sink into the soft ground. Can you believe it? And then there were the other applications, for the erection of loose-boxes and coach houses, the establishment of a caravan site, the restoration of a war-damaged building, the improvement of a private road . . . I tell you, they're endless.'

Arnold glanced towards the file; it seemed thick. 'Were any of the applications successful?'

'None. You would have assumed old Willington would have won *something*, wouldn't you? But half of them were withdrawn, anyway. Change of circumstances, he said. Change of mind, really. A grasshopper.'

The Senior Planning Officer had still not delineated the problem, Arnold considered. Almost as though he had caught the fleeting thought, the Senior Planning Officer scowled again. 'He's got another bloody application in. I want you to take it up. Get out there, find out what it's all about and—'

He had no time to say more. There was a discreet tap on the door, it opened, and a nervous clerk peeked around. She hesitated. 'Are you expecting two gentlemen . . . ?'

'Mr Wilson and Mr Livingstone,' the Senior Planning Officer said and rose from his chair. The girl bobbed her head, disappeared and a few moments later two men were ushered into the room.

'Ah, Mr Wilson,' the Senior Planning Officer said, extending his hand, 'nice to see you again. This is my colleague, Mr Arnold Landon.'

Wilson was a middle-sized, middle-aged man in a grey, herringbone suit. His handclasp was hard and purposeful, with an element of curiosity in it as though testing for strength. There was a certain frostiness in his smile that suggested caution, and his eyes were as flat as a frozen lake, grey under an afternoon sky. 'Mr Landon,' he acknowledged briefly, and his tone was dismissive. In a few seconds he had summed up Arnold and concluded he would be of no interest. He would see only a lean, middle-aged man with thinning, greying hair and a wispy, ineffectual moustache dominated by a nose that jutted like a piece of weathered timber from a sunburned face. Arnold's baggy, worn brown suit was in sharp contrast to the Senior Planning Officer's neat grey smartness and he was a man to he discounted.

The Senior Planning Officer was turning with an ingratiating smile to the second man. 'You must be Mr Livingstone . . . I *presume*?'

There was a weary acceptance in Livingstone's intelligent eyes as he suffered the Senior Planning Officer's inane comment. He was taller, younger and more muscular than his companion. His reddish hair had receded at the temples, giving him the look of an academic, but there was a controlled force about his body that suggested much more athletic pursuits. He moved lightly on his feet, and his grip when he shook hands was light, noncommittal, as he made his own summaries. He stared at Arnold; his glance was vague, as though he was flicking over in his mind the pages of a book, concentrating not on the present, but on distant events. 'Landon,' he murmured. 'Haven't we met before? The name . . .'

'I think not,' Arnold said self-effacingly, aware of the displeased glance from the Senior Planning Officer. They could both guess what was coming, and neither welcomed it.

Livingstone's brow furrowed with thought, then slowly he nodded. 'No, we haven't met. But I've heard of you, I think. Aren't you the Arnold Landon who's an expert on mediaeval buildings and that sort of thing?'

That sort of thing. It was, Arnold supposed, one way of explaining the passion in his life. Unqualified for work in planning as a result of a lack of formal education, he had ended eight boring years in the Town Clerk's department simply because it had become known he was a queer chap who seemed to know everything there was to know about wood, and building materials . . . and things like that. It had been the decision of the Senior Planning Officer to arrange his transfer: there had been occasions since, as publicity had hummed about the department, when the Senior Planning Officer had seriously regretted that decision.

Livingstone was still appraising him carefully. 'There was something fairly recently, wasn't there? In the papers, something to do with a killing, Oakham Manor in Northumberland, was that it?'

'Mr Landon,' the Senior Planning Officer intervened firmly, 'has had certain unfortunate experiences but they are nothing to do with the workings of this office. Please, gentlemen, won't you sit down? And some coffee? We have a vending machine in the corridor—'

Both men demurred, a trifle hastily. They were clearly used to something better than machine-made coffee. Or maybe, Arnold reflected, they wanted no involvement with the prime exhibit in a lawsuit.

The Senior Planning Officer was settling himself behind his desk once more. He steepled his hands, inspecting the fingertips, and smiled in mysterious fashion. 'I trust . . . ah . . . business is going well for both of you?'

'Well enough,' Wilson said.

'And actively enough to make us both wish to conclude business here with despatch,' Livingstone added coolly.

'Ah yes, of course,' the Senior Planning Officer said, flustered. 'I merely meant . . . the courtesies . . .' He collected himself, flushing slightly. 'Mr Landon, ah, the reason I've asked Mr Landon to be present here to meet you two gentlemen is because with pressure of work in the office it's necessary that I should hand over the responsibility for processing your application to him. It had been my intention to deal with it myself, but I have leave due to me, I am aware you wish early decisions to be made by the planning committee, and so it seemed to me that Mr Landon—'

'Fine,' Wilson cut in. 'So we've met your Mr Landon. He'll be handling the application. And now we've met. So . . . ?'

The Senior Planning Officer unsteepled his hands. 'Ah. Well. Fact is, your papers are being processed, but in any application like this it's wise to have the . . . ah . . . background explained. Things can arise at the committee which are, shall we say, unexpected? Opposition can come from unlikely quarters. We don't enjoy . . . difficult meetings. The Chairman, for instance, he likes to have a quiet meeting. Things are so much more civilized that way. And it makes things so much smoother for us, as well. So, since Mr Landon will be handling the paperwork and, as responsible officer, will need to make recommendations to the committee, it would perhaps be wise . . .'

'I can fill him in on the background,' Livingstone said.

He smiled. He had good teeth and the smile was easy, lending charm to his features. He knew it, of course, and Arnold was not fooled by it, but if it helped ease situations that was fine. Wilson remained tight-lipped and cautious, but his companion was clearly at ease.

'The situation is this,' Livingstone said, leaning forward in his chair and engaging Arnold with an earnest glance. 'Just north of Darras Hall, some twelve miles inside the boundary of the county, there's a place called Penbrook Farm.'

Arnold nodded slowly, considering in his mind's eye the map of the county he held in his office. 'I think I know it.'

'It's not up to much as a farm,' Livingstone went on. 'I guess in the old days, maybe thirty, forty years ago, it was a better proposition, but the old dear who holds it now she's not really capable of developing it properly or even keeping it going. Most of the fields are fallow; there's very little livestock — a few sheep, I think—'

'None of your Chillingham herds and that sort of thing,' the Senior Planning Officer offered supportively.

Livingstone ignored him 'The location of the farm is interesting. The main farmhouse — which is a bit ramshackle now — is built on a hillside overlooking some meadows, a meandering sort of stream, and then the ground rises to some fairly extensive woodland. Not valuable trees, you understand, Just scrub, alder, a few Scots pine, rubbish really, but . . . environmentally attractive.'

The words had been used deliberately, and soothingly.

The calculating Mr Livingstone, Arnold guessed, would be far more interested in profit than environment.

'Behind the trees there's something like another fifteen acres of land. Not worth much at all; granite outcrops, broken ground. You know the kind of area I mean.' Arnold knew. Much of it was fast disappearing as housing demands spread out from Newcastle and Morpeth.

'Then, across the river, there's about another eighty acres of flat land and that's about the whole thing. That particular area doesn't form part of Penbrook Farm, though it does actually figure in our general plans.'

Arnold could already guess the answer but he asked the question anyway. 'Who owns that land?'

Livingstone shrugged. 'A business consortium.'

'And you have an interest?'

Livingstone hesitated, glanced at Wilson and then said stonily, 'Mr Wilson and I are shareholders, yes. There are others involved also.'

Arnold nodded. He was aware of the Senior Planning Officer watching him carefully. 'What exactly do your proposals comprise, then?'

'It's like this,' Livingstone replied. 'Penbrook Farm is worked out. It's never going to amount to anything again. The owner is an old lady who's never displayed much interest in the farm as a working proposition. We aim to . . . renovate the whole situation.'

'*Renovate*?'

Livingstone nodded. 'If you think about the situation you'll understand the possibilities. Penbrook Farm lies just north of one of the most expensive, stockbroker-type housing developments in the North-East. Not ten miles north-east of the farm is Morpeth, county headquarters. Okay, so the whole area of the North-East is tight in the middle of economic depression, but curiously enough it's also a place where there are still big pockets of real money.'

'I still don't see—'

'We're proposing to build an old people's home at Penbrook Farm.'

The intervention came, impatiently, from Wilson. His tone was cold and dispassionate. He took out a cigarette case from his inside pocket and lit a cigarette. In the silence Arnold stared at him disbelievingly. 'An old people's home?' he repeated.

'Just that.' Wilson's ice-cold eyes watched the smoke rise from his cigarette for a few seconds and then he stared at Arnold. The indifference was complete. 'We intend calling it the Minford Twilight Home.'

Arnold stared at Wilson for several seconds. Incomprehension had dulled his senses. Slowly, something cold crawled in his stomach as the name bit home. 'Minford?'

'That's right.' Wilson was aware of the surprise in Arnold's tone but was unmoved by it. 'The Minford Twilight Home. You'll know Councillor Minford, I imagine.'

Arnold had never met Albert Minford but knew of him. He had been active as a councillor for a decade or more. He had acquired sufficient wealth from the business his father had built to be able to regard politics as an appropriate substitute for a career. It was rumoured he was hungry for the accolade that had never yet come from Buckingham Palace; talk was he was still expecting an honour, and this accounted for much of the charity work he was seen to be active in. He was not averse to accepting the odd local honour, however: when he did a stint as chairman of the local education committee he had been pleased to have a secondary school named after him, and there had also been the Minford Hospital Wing to be proud of after he had organized a charitable appeal some five years ago.

'I've heard of Councillor Minford. He's never served on planning, so I've never actually met him. I wasn't aware he was active on Welfare, either.'

Wilson contemplated the glowing end of his cigarette. 'So?'

'Well, if there is a proposal to name the home after him . . . unless . . . is he a member of your consortium?'

Livingstone stirred, Arnold thought somewhat uneasily, but Wilson merely looked at the Senior Planning Officer. Arnold's superior shook his head. 'No, that's not so. Perish the mere thought, Arnold. It would be . . . unethical, in my view, were that to be the case.'

Wilson smiled thinly. 'We have decided to name the new home after Councillor Minford merely in admiration for the unstinting way in which he has served the community in his capacity as councillor. The county should be proud of his efforts, and it seems to us, as businessmen involved in the community, that the gesture would be an appropriate one.'

A short silence fell. Arnold felt as though he had been snubbed. The Senior Planning Officer contemplated his fingernails. Arnold cleared his throat. 'I see . . . May I ask, then, what the planning application comprises?'

Wilson's glance lingered over Arnold for a few moments, then slipped towards Livingstone. At the almost imperceptible nod of permission, Livingstone said, 'Clearly, you'll need to familiarize yourself with the situation.'

'Clearly.'

'There's a great deal of work to be done.'

'Of course.'

'We are aware there are certain members of the planning committee who will wish to go into matters in some detail,' Livingstone said. 'We are fairly certain there will be crucial questions concerning the location of the home.'

'Opposition, you mean?'

A faint flush of annoyance stained Livingstone's features. 'We wouldn't say opposition. It's merely that certain members of the committee will, we guess, wish to be assured that there are no problems with regard to the location matter. It's as well that you should be aware — in case you are asked by the committee — of the total picture regarding the application. The Minford Home will be an ideal last resting place for the elderly — peace, quiet, the Northumberland countryside, easy access to both Newcastle and Morpeth, with the sweep of the hinterland to enjoy, and distant scents of the sea . . . We are confident that Penbrook Farm, for these reasons, is the perfect location for such an enterprise.'

The presentation brief had already been prepared, Arnold thought cynically. 'Its location may be ideal, but I would have thought access was not that easy with winding country roads—'

'Ah, we have to admit,' Livingstone interrupted, smiling easily, 'there will be much work to be done. At considerable expense. Our expense. Road widening and improvement schemes will form part of the planning application. There's a diversion arrangement we'll need to have approved, a drainage scheme, a change of use for certain of the adjoining farm properties which are presently leased — but we've also built into the proposal certain conditions which we're quite happy to have imposed on us, relating to the preservation of trees and woodlands . . .' Livingstone gave another winning smile. 'We've taken the best advice.'

Arnold hesitated, then took a deep breath. 'This all sounds . . . most philanthropic, but you'll forgive me for saying there must be a catch somewhere.'

The Senior Planning Officer frowned. 'Catch? Arnold, it's not our business to—'

'No, that's all right.' Livingstone held up a placatory hand, and twisted his smile into a grimace. 'We're businessmen, we admit it. Mr Wilson and I, and our associates, do have certain commitments here in this project — to old people, to the environment — but it would be less than honest to suggest we didn't have other irons in this particular fire as well. Service roads, access, the location itself, a fine place for a home for elderly people; but it's also a natural high class housing development which can serve the mobile business population of the area. We know already, for instance, that two of the major American companies who have executives in the district would be more than interested in acquiring high-cost, easily saleable properties in such an area. There's the possibility of a country house because of the proximity of the moors, with shooting rights below the Cheviot. Yes, we admit there are strong business considerations we have taken into account.'

The Senior Planning Officer had steepled his fingers again. His eyes were no longer on Arnold. He was contemplating his desk as though he had never seen it before. He was the independent, objective, uncommitted planning officer. All decisions in such matters were made by politicians: he was simply a servant.

'Such a development would need planning permission, for a change of use in agricultural land—'

'Which is at present largely derelict,' Livingstone supplied.

'And the farm—'

'It's possible a compulsory purchase order will have to be made against the owner of Penbrook Farm,' Wilson said harshly.

'These are high hurdles you've set yourselves,' Arnold suggested. 'A planning inquiry could be demanded, and the Minister—'

'Is unlikely to intervene,' Wilson shrugged.

'I beg to differ,' Arnold said warmly. 'In so many cases like these, public protests—'

Livingstone cleared his throat. 'In this particular situation we are fairly confident that the political will is strong enough to carry through the proposals without a planning inquiry.'

'The price being an old people's home?' Arnold asked disbelievingly.

'The *Minford* Twilight Home,' Livingstone corrected him gently.

Arnold sat back in his chair. He stared at the two men facing him: Livingstone was still at ease, confident in his control of the situation; Wilson smoked his cigarette indifferently, aware there was nothing in this room to fear. Their plans had been made, their commitments determined, their paths cleared of possible debris, and Arnold was quite sure they were quite sure they could get what they wanted. He was not very happy about it. He glanced at the Senior Planning Officer for confirmation of any kind, but his superior merely shifted in his seat and gestured towards the manila folder in front of him. 'The details of the planning and compulsory purchase applications are here, Arnold. I think it's an appropriate time for us to go into these in some detail now. It will familiarize you with the whole situation before I go on leave. You can take it from there afterwards. Perhaps you'd like to start, Mr Livingstone? While you're settling the basic details with Mr Landon, I'll nip out and get us all a cup of coffee. Each.'

Before anyone could utter a word of protest, he drifted purposefully from the room.

2

Working in the Town Clerk's department had been stifling for a man who had been brought up in the Yorkshire Dales, with a father who had tramped with him through the valleys and across the fells, showed him the decayed villages, traced for him the remnants of a long-dead time.

In the planning department it was different for he had reason and excuse to get out into the crisp morning air, travel the winding roads of Northumbria, smell the tang of the distant sea and in summertime watch the shimmering dance of the Cheviot, blue above Rothbury and the Coquet.

Three days after the meeting in the Senior Planning Officer's room, Arnold had got rid of enough paperwork to be able to undertake the tasks the Senior Planning Officer had left him before he took his leave, inevitably, in Scarborough. Arnold decided to make a day of it. The morning could be spent visiting Willington Hall; the afternoon, on a return journey that would take him not too far from his own home outside Morpeth, could be spent at Penbrook Farm.

The journey was deliberately planned. It meant that, since Willington Hall was located in the wild eastern hinterland of the county, close to the Cumbrian border, he could take the drive from Morpeth towards the old military road.

For Arnold, it was a perfect morning for such a drive. He left early, knowing that west of Housesteads he would have the autumn winds to cleanse his lungs while he contemplated the hard times the Roman sentries must have experienced as guardians of the northern frontier, Hadrian's Wall. He was early enough to be able to afford a halt at Crag Lough Wood. He sat on a granite outcrop and watched the wind shaking the pines as though it was desperate to hurl them into the lough below, where white horses danced against the reedy shores and a thin mist of spray drifted up over the heather-covered slopes.

Those Roman soldiers and architects had been canny men: it was easy to see why they built their wall here, across the frozen throat of Britain. The granite hills, rolling northwards, fell sheer at the stark, petrified wave of Whin Sill rock. The thin snake of the wall itself crawled over the crests — east over King's Hill to Carrawburgh, west by way of Cuddy's Crags to Steel Rigg and the Nine Nicks of Thirlwall.

But the Wilsons and the Livingstones of this modern time were canny men too, in their own way. They knew where they were driving, and they knew how to do it. They knew where the productive places were and they knew how to protect their backs against alien spears. But while Arnold felt he could relate to the empire-building Roman generals, he was entirely out of sympathy with the businessmen who were set to build their own little empires. It was a paradox; perhaps it was only distance and time that made the difference, and he guessed that it might be the same entrepreneurial drive that had motivated those long-dead generals and the new business captains. He could not tell.

Even so, the machinations of Wilson and Livingstone and the politicians in their pockets bothered him.

Such machinations, he reasoned as he left Crag Lough Wood shouldn't really bother him. He should react as he was supposed to react, as a servant of the council, a humble planning officer. He had no hand in policy-making, no points of view to put that should be divorced from fact. An adviser on practical matters, nothing more.

Yet he knew, as he drove west, that he could not change. To the south towards the Durham hills that served as a backdrop, he could see the last traces of General Wade's old military road. The shafts of sunlight that raked across the valley of the South Tyne were bleak and cheerless, presaging little other than a sequel of black cloud, squalling furiously across the valley slopes. A townsman might shiver deep into his raincoat, but Arnold saw only grandeur and the power of the air and the earth. Fanciful; yet realistic.

The Wilsons and the Livingstones came and went.

The problem was, while they lived, they could do so much damage.

* * *

Arnold drove on. The land lifted, rising until, to the north, he could see the dark distant cohorts of Forestry Commission pinewoods that had already altered the landscape of bracken and bentwoods that would otherwise have been recognizable to the Brigantians of fifteen hundred years ago. He glanced at his watch; he had calculated he would be at Willington Hall by ten o'clock. He should soon be reaching the crossroads, and the sign that would direct him to Estley village and beyond, the Hall itself.

At last the road began to drop, carpeting pinewoods appearing ahead of him, and as it did so the sky lightened, patches of blue emerging against the grey, spreading, extending until the autumn sunshine was warm through the car window.

The tiny hamlet of Estley went by. Dating from about 1500, the church there was of little interest, except for the unusual ashlared hardstone used in its construction. The road narrowed thereafter, and its surface degenerated. The fields he passed through seemed exhausted; there was a general air of depression in the area, heightened by ruined barns, a weathered folly on the skyline, a tumbled sheep pen on the fern-withered slopes.

When he reached Willington Hall, Arnold was appalled. He came upon it suddenly, unexpectedly.

It was the way the house would have been planned, perhaps three centuries ago. The shoulder of the hill curved away to the left and the road swung out of the trees to give a view across a small vale, sheltering under mist-shrouded hills. The Hall sat squarely at the base of the hill where at one time it might have twinkled in the sunshine, warm magnesian limestone sparkling after a shower of rain, fresh hewn and crystalline. Its south front had been grand, the two wings curving slightly like bull's horns, protecting the broad terrace and the sweep of the steps, and the meadows below the terrace had sloped above the gently meandering stream to provide a smooth view to rising slopes beyond.

Now, all had changed.

The east wing had crumbled and taken on the appearance of a Victorian folly, its crenellations the result of depredations of rain and wind. At some time, repairs had been carried out but inferior stone had been used and the limestone had changed in colour to a dull, drab grey. Even from this distance Arnold could guess at the sponginess of the stone. Along the east front it was worse — a flaky dust where the chemicals of the atmosphere had eaten into the surface of the stone.

He drove down into the vale and his heart sank.

The bridge across which he drove showed signs of senility: the handrails sagged, desperately clinging to their supports to avoid the plunge into a stream that had been fouled for years, weed-ridden and dank. The meadows beyond were rank, clotted with weed and unproductive, their richness dissipated, deserted even by summer butterflies. The broad steps that led up to the terrace were green with lichen; the limestone had been badly patched with sandstone and the consequent chemical reaction between the materials had led to rapid decay.

So it was with the Hall itself. The whole fabric of the building was at risk, *had been* at risk for two decades and more.

The depredations of time, the weathering of wind and rain had destroyed the facade, eating into the stone and crumbling its splendour into decay.

Tears prickled at the back of Arnold Landon's eyes. He could not explain the emotion, and yet he was aware that the building still had a splendour that decay could not erase, a grandeur that the negligence of its owners could not destroy. Men had built it, but it had drawn around itself a mantle of history that, now, it would retain in spite of the erosion of time. It was an old man, clothed with dignity in spite of poverty and the beckoning of time.

And yet he could have cried.

* * *

The building was reflected in the man.

Patrick Willington was in his late sixties. He was a tall, desiccated individual whose hollowed eyes hinted at desperations he had thought he'd conquered forty years ago. His skin had a yellowed tinge, like parchment exposed to a light unfamiliar; his mouth was thin-lipped, so that the reedy voice came as no surprise. There was something in his nervous movements that suggested to Arnold the blind commitments of a fanatic, and his hands were as confident as an architect's, subtle in their movement, precise in their decision. He belonged to a time that was past in that he was gentle of speech, mannerly, concerned about the impressions he might convey. He was *genteel.*

And he had never known Willington Hall.

Arnold could not be certain at what point of time he had reached that conclusion. There was the evidence of the building itself, of course, quite apart from the grounds. But it was more subtle than that. Patrick Willington had lived at Willington Hall most of his life and yet he had never really *seen* it, never appreciated what it was and had been, never recognized what it had become. What existed in his own retinal conclusions was far divorced from the reality; perhaps his recollections of his family and its place in history were equally unreal.

'We have been here for a long time, of course, Mr Landon. You'll have heard of the Willingtons of Willington, naturally. Like so many of the landed gentry our origins are, shall we say, somewhat scented? Edward Willington was an administrator in Calcutta in the 1750s and did quite well, becoming a member of the council of Bengal. Warren Hastings's finances were in an appalling state of course, but old Edward helped out a lot there, organizing the opium revenue. He came back in 1784 quite a rich man. It was he who renovated the east wing of the Hall, you know — interesting to think opium paid for that. Passed the rest of his life at Willington Hall — he gave it the name — as a country gentleman.'

Standing at the long window of the library, he gestured vaguely, limp-wristed, towards the sour meadows below them. 'Old Edward was interested in it all, but there was trouble with his sons, and at the time of the Napoleonic Wars quite a lot of stuff was stripped out, for some obscure reason that escapes me. It was Charles Willington who extended the farmland in the 1840s, and his son William who changed the course of the stream in 1882. He was a lawyer, you know, and change was in the air for lawyers in the 1880s. He was infected by it. My father, sadly, was infected with something quite different: like my grandfather, he was addicted to chorus girls — though neither married one — and they tended to support their predilections by taking money from the property, and doing nothing to replace it.'

Patrick Willington was proud to explain to Arnold that his own attitudes to the estate had been quite different. 'I was a major in the war, you know, and saw some terrible things. Coming back to Willington was . . . like fulfilling a dream. I determined to stay here, build the place up again. There was a problem, of course.'

'The bad winter of 1947?' Arnold asked.

The old man glanced at him vaguely, turning away from the window. 'The winter? Oh no, I mean that was a blow, of course, decimated our sheep. No, there was a family problem. There were just the two of us, you see, my sister and I. I always thought we got on quite well, but she had a funny streak. Never realized her sense of . . . *position*, don't you know? There was a chap, lived down at the village . . . when I got back from the army I heard she'd taken up with him, and we had some violent words about it and I forbade her. Anyway she took it all rather badly, and had the vapours, you know the way young women are.' His hollowed eyes clouded suddenly, misted by the passage of time and the vagueness of memory, and he seemed to be searching for something that eluded him after all these years. He shook his head. It eluded him still. 'Could never understand it, really. I mean, she took it so *actively*, you know what I mean? Refused to speak to me, sneaked off to meet the feller, all that sort of thing . . .'

His glance strayed to the windows and he paused. 'Out here, you know, with an estate like Willington, there are responsibilities. Family. They have to accept those kind of responsibilities. She didn't. Sneaking off like that. Henry now, my son, he's different. Always looking to the day when he would inherit Willington. In his blood. Longs for the day when he could get to manage it . . . bit headstrong, the young are, so I've kept him on a tight rein — I admit it — but it's for his own good, you know? But my sister, she was of a different vein. And when that feller came on the land, and I caught him, I did what any brother would do. Odd, that, she never forgave me. And she knew how to hurt; knew where to strike. Took from me my dearest possession . . .'

Arnold felt vaguely embarrassed. He had the impression that Patrick Willington was hardly aware of his presence any longer, but was contemplating a past that had become distant and unimportant, until dredged up by chance, as now.

'Still,' Patrick Willington said, as though picking up Arnold's thoughts, 'it's all of little consequence now. After that row she up and went, most surprisingly. Always thought her a mouse. But she left, went to Scotland or somewhere. She had some money of her own . . . Mother left it to her. I could have used that money . . . sunk it into the estate, maybe turned the place around with it. But she left, and somehow . . . there was a period when I looked for her, she'd taken to wandering . . . Europe . . .' His brow became furrowed, the desiccated skin stretched tight over his cheekbones as he foraged for reasons half forgotten. 'Never found her. Bad business. The wrong she did, it's never left me, but haven't seen hide nor hair of her since, so what's the odds?' His brow cleared as unpleasant memories departed. 'Bit of cash then would have made a difference, but I managed. Dragged the estate into the twentieth century. Tried to make the farms profitable. Improved the drainage in the lower fields. Upgraded stock. Brought in new strains.'

'Government subsidies—'

'Took advantage of those, naturally. Won't pretend it's not been hard work. But rewarding.'

Arnold thought about the sour fields he had seen on the approach to Willington Hall. He was fascinated by Patrick Willington's inability to perceive the reality about him. He seemed to feel all was well, and he had kept the estate going, but in Arnold's view, if the man could be applauded for his commitment to the land he could hardly be admired for his efficiency in managing it.

'We had appallingly bad luck, of course. I mean, the upkeep of the Hall itself has been crippling, and there was bad weather, the poor harvests, and the personnel . . . I mean before Henry came home I had a young chap who was making a perfect hash of things, so I took over entirely from him, and when Henry's been long enough on the estate to understand, well, maybe I'll let him have a free hand.'

Not this side of the grave, Arnold thought.

The old man began to cough and his yellowish skin took on a transparency that emphasized his frailty. 'My new scheme, it will give us the chance to turn things around . . .'

It was to be a sawmill. Patrick Willington's application had seemed unrealistic when Arnold had looked at it in the office, but now the old man attempted to describe it and Arnold became more than ever convinced that the owner of

Willington Hall had no more business sense than farming acumen. It seemed to Arnold that everything was against the project. As far as the estate itself was concerned, the woodland was thin and little that could be regarded as marketable grew there; much had been stripped away over the years. So a sawmill would have no immediate source of timber to start business. Secondly, the isolation of the Hall itself would surely mean that the likelihood of business coming to it would be remote. Even if there was work in the area, the access roads were hardly suitable for heavy traffic. Besides, to Arnold's knowledge there were at least two sawmills with spare capacity located within twenty miles of Willington Hall, and both were far more accessible, with main road situations.

'Are you sure this mill would be a paying proposition?' Arnold asked cautiously. He spoke with care because, strictly speaking, it was none of his business. As planning officer his concern was mainly with environmental matters, not with the likely profitability — or otherwise — of the scheme. As far as he could ascertain, Patrick Willington would be throwing money away over this scheme, money he could ill afford if one took into account the general state of Willington Hall.

'It will be a turning-point for the estate,' Patrick Willington enthused, 'and I look forward to the building once the application is approved. Now then, Mr Landon, a little dry sherry before you leave?'

* * *

Arnold left the crumbling terrace of Willington Hall with a feeling of despondency. The great estates of Northumberland still flourished, a High Tory fiefdom of ancestral parks and stately houses, discreetly hidden behind great avenues of sturdy trees. The farms were fat, the generous fields had still not lost their hedgerow oaks. But there were the Willington Halls too, the struggling manors where money had run out, where crippling death duties had taken their toll, and where mismanagement over decades had stripped the land of its richness until the houses themselves decayed, showed gaunt rib-trees to the sky and rain, and slipped into a graceless desuetude. Arnold bled for the waste and the sadness of it all.

He made his way back to the car, and was hardly aware of the man standing there until he was almost upon him.

'Morning.'

He was dressed in a leather-patched jacket and corduroy trousers and his boots were splashed with mud. The knotted scarf he wore at his throat had loosened and the skin there was as wind-tanned as his face and hands. He was about thirty-five years old but his fair hair was receding, thinning at the temples, and there were lines on his face that suggested he had concerns beyond his years. His eyes were a pale brown, lacking the softness of a darker hue, and somehow lacking in emotion. Arnold felt he was being subjected to a steady, cold appraisal and he found the thought disconcerting.

Arnold returned the greeting and began to unlock his car door. The man rested an arm on the roof of Arnold's car. 'You been to see my father?'

Young Henry, Patrick had called him. Arnold looked at the heir to Willington Hall with more interest. 'That's right. My name's Landon. I'm a planning officer, based at Morpeth.'

Henry Willington frowned vaguely. 'You come about the application regarding the sawmill?'

'That's right.'

'Bloody nonsense.'

Arnold was inclined to agree. He studied Henry Willington for a moment and then asked, 'Can't you persuade him to drop it?'

'Will it go through planning?'

'It's possible.'

Henry Willington grunted in dissatisfaction. 'No, I can't persuade him to drop it. He may be an old man but he's stubborn as hell as far as Willington is concerned. He thinks he knows what's best for the estate, in spite of all the evidence of his mismanagement that's staring him in the face. This isn't the first hare-brained scheme he's had, Mr Landon.'

'I understand,' Arnold said quietly, 'that there have been quite a few applications over the years.'

'A *few*!' Henry Willington snorted. 'That's an understatement. You know, the whole thing is crazy. I was eighteen when I was sent away — at some expense — to Seale Hayne Agricultural College. I came back with all the theory, and some good ideas. But my education was a waste of time. He never listened to a thing I said. Still doesn't. It would have been possible, maybe ten years ago, to turn this place around. Now, I'm not so sure. God knows why I still hang on.'

'You manage the estate, I understand.'

'Is that what he said?' Henry Willington said bitterly. 'Well, maybe it's so, in name. We've few staff anyway, and not much by way of stock, and the farms are leased out, so it's not much to manage at all. But he still does everything himself, even keeping the books, though I have to rewrite every damn one of them afterwards. He'll have told you how his father and grandfather ruined Willington. At least they had a purpose in their negligence, and they enjoyed themselves. But my father — he's just seeing the place down the drain. *Actively*. Can he get much pleasure out of that?'

Arnold hesitated. 'I think perhaps he isn't aware . . .'

'Damn right he isn't.' Henry Willington's fists clenched suddenly, and Arnold was aware of the frustration, coiled like a snake inside the man. 'And it's all gone too far now. Death duties will rip apart what's left of this place, and why the hell I stay on . . .'

Arnold could guess. Brought up at the Hall, Henry would find it difficult to tear himself away from the decaying estates. Hoping, perhaps, that there could be a retrieval of fortunes, a turnaround of the finance, a return to better days. It would be a forlorn hope, and Henry Willington would know it. 'I'd better be going,' Arnold said.

Henry Willington's pale brown eyes were fixed on his. 'I don't want this application going through. If he spends — *wastes* — any more money on stupid schemes . . .'

'I don't really have much control over the matter.'

'You're the planning officer. You'll advise the committee.'

'That's all. Advice.'

'But you know it's crazy.'

Arnold nodded slowly. 'I don't think it'll work.'

Henry Willington held his glance for a long moment. Then he made a humphing sound, nodded, and stepped away from the car, apparently satisfied. And yet, Arnold thought, in the end nothing will satisfy Henry Willington other than the resurrection of the Willington estates as a manageable property. Which meant the likelihood of his ever being satisfied was remote.

* * *

Arnold's mood of despondency did not fade until he had left Willington Hall way behind him. The morning was all but over now, but the sky had lightened, wintry patches of blue appearing above the hills. He had brought a Thermos flask of coffee and some sandwiches with him and he stopped on a piece of open ground, with a burn tumbling to his left, to have a sparse lunch.

A day out of the office like this was good. Willington Hall had been depressing, but at least Arnold was out in the open air, by himself. Penbrook Farm, his next point of call, was some thirty miles distant but it would be a pleasant drive over the looping fell road, and now the sky was brightening he would get splendid views across the North Tyne to the Durham hills.

He finished his lunch, relaxed for half an hour, just listening to the burn, and then he drove on. He arrived at Penbrook Farm in the early afternoon.

He entered the gate at the north end of the property and the fields lay spread below him. To his left was a copse of hazel with, to his surprise, a scattering of standard oaks. In front of him the land fell away, the fields neatly hedgerowed, and there was something about the pattern that affected him, a feeling of *déjà vu*, an emotion stirring inside him that reminded him of his childhood, walking in the broad-leaved woods with his father. He sat there, silent, looking at the fields, and the stream that straggled its way along the eastern boundary, the greening tiles of the roof of the farmhouse, the slow ascent of blue smoke from the chimney and the clump of the old barn beyond.

There was a lump in his throat, the prickle of tears at the back of his eyes and he could not understand why. Then he heard the tapping at the car window and he turned his head.

Inches from his face was the threatening muzzle of a double-barrelled shotgun.

3

The woman was in her early fifties. She had a woollen cap crammed on her head, from which a few greying, untidy curls escaped in a ragged fringe. A thick muffler protected her throat and the tweed jacket she wore had seen better days even before thorn and rain had further dilapidated it. Her woollen gloves had been cut off at the knuckles to leave her fingers free: they were red and wind-chapped, but the grip on the shotgun was fierce, and the pouched eyes in the heavy, folded face glittered with determined passion.

Arnold wound down the window with an exaggerated care.

'Don't get out, mister. You can reverse to the gate. Then I just want to see the back of you, going like hell down the road.'

There was a guttural Northumbrian catch in her throat, and her accent was Border Country, and yet there was something about it that suggested to Arnold not an affectation but a deliberate attempt to communicate. Her accent was adopted, but her intention was clear enough.

'Excuse me, but—'

'No excuse me. Just get off Penbrook.'

'You are . . . ?'

'The hell with who I am. *Get off this property*!'

Arnold expelled his breath slowly. The wicked mouths of the twin barrels were pointed unwaveringly at his head, eager to explode, and his stomach seemed to have sunk, his legs beginning to tremble uncontrollably. He swallowed hard and said insistently, 'Are you the owner of Penbrook Farm?'

For a moment silence fell, and the gun barrels wavered slightly. The eyes were unremitting, however. 'No matter. I told you. Get off the farm.'

'I'm sorry, but I have a job to do.' Arnold's tone was firm even though his mouth was dry with fear. 'And I need to—'

'You hired by those bastards Wilson and Livingstone?'

The eyes darted suspicion and malice at him and the nose was wrinkled in distaste. Arnold blinked. 'Wilson and . . . er . . . Livingstone? Look, I'm employed by the local authority. I'm a planning officer, based at Morpeth, my name's Landon and I've come in respect of an application—'

He stopped as the barrels were suddenly lowered. The woman stepped back, uncertainly, staring at him with the same suspicion, but overlaid now with doubt. 'Planning? You come to weigh up cases?'

'Something like that,' Arnold replied in relief.

Silence fell between them. The woman took another step backwards. He could see her more clearly now, dumpy, middle-aged, clad in a calf-length black woollen skirt and gumboots, less menacing than previously, the shotgun drooping with uncertainty in her hands.

'Planning,' she said thoughtfully, then in a sharp action broke the barrel of the shotgun. 'You'll need to talk to Sarah.' She paused, gestured down towards the farmhouse in the hollow. 'She's down there.'

'Thank you.'

The woman snorted impatiently and moved away towards the screen of hazel coppice from which she had earlier emerged. 'I'll see you down there . . . My name's SauvageBrown.'

She turned, making surprisingly little disturbance in the undergrowth as she ploughed her way into the trees. In seconds she had disappeared. Arnold sat silently in the car, staring after her.

Mildred Sauvage-Brown.

The Senior Planning Officer possessed language of considerable colour and invective. When he was disturbed he indulged in it. When he was deeply disturbed, and consistently disturbed, he controlled his language in that respect but the control was more effective for all that.

'Mildred Sauvage-Brown,' he had once said firmly to Arnold, 'is a violent pain in the backside.'

The conviction in the Senior Planning Officer's tone had persuaded Arnold that Miss Sauvage-Brown would be worth looking up. A view of the scattered files and some discreet inquiries had given him the information he desired. She had never crossed Arnold's path, but most of the rest of the planning staff had bruises to prove the acquaintance.

She was a curiosity.

Her father had been a second-generation German immigrant in the United States. Her mother had been an Englishwoman of rather more than modest means. Mr Braun had anglicized his name upon his marriage and when Mildred was born in New York she had been endowed with a hyphenated surname that ensured remembrance of her mother's considerable social status in Hampshire, England.

Mildred had come to England in the last year of the war and had never returned. The clothing business run by Mr Braun and the money left to her by her mother had ensured she was well placed to indulge herself in England. Her indulgence had been supported by beliefs, nurtured by her mother that old England was worth preserving, and by character, epitomized by Germano-American persistence and stubbornness that broke through in numerous lawsuits, inquiries and tribunal hearings in Suffolk and Hampshire during the 1950s.

Evidently she had decided the South was, eventually, not worth preserving, for in the sixties she had come north, fallen in love with the Border Country and transplanted her affection. The roots had grown sturdy, deep and strong, and had, according to the Senior Planning Officer, strangled many a planning project at birth. He had grudgingly admitted that the country needed people like her, but not too often, and in not too great a number.

And Mildred Sauvage-Brown was here on Penbrook Farm.

For a moment, Arnold felt a twinge of sympathy for Mr Wilson and Mr Livingstone. Then he started the car and drove on down the hill.

The farm was interesting. On the hillside above the hollow there was a woodland of ash, elm and small-leaved lime trees. A spinney of thorn hung on the craggy edge of the hill and along to his right as he drove the twisting track he caught a glimpse of the squat stubs of old pollards. They would once have served as woodland boundary markers, and a small knot of warm excitement began to gather in his chest.

The track swung sharp left and he slowed as he came level with the barn, a fifteenth-century structure, he guessed. Beyond the barn was a pigsty, and then the farmhouse itself. It could not boast the lineage of the barn: there would probably have been an old farmhouse on the site, but from its appearance Arnold guessed that the older building would have been demolished near the turn of the century because this structure was certainly no older than the 1890s.

He found difficulty parking his car; there was a muddy Range Rover parked across the track and a battered Austin in the yard beyond. Arnold reversed slowly, turned, and edged his way back up the track so that he would be able to leave the farm more easily after his interview with the owner. He cut the engine, got out of the car and locked it. He was parked some twenty yards from the pigsty.

It was a nondescript enough construction. The sty itself was squared, built of limestone which had weathered to a dull, drab grey, lichen-stained and crumbled badly in one corner. The pen beyond was perhaps five feet high, again of limestone, and part of the roof had fallen in, with the eastern corner repaired, badly enough, with corrugated iron. But enough of the original roof remained to interest Arnold. He walked across to the sty and looked at it more closely.

He was still standing there when Mildred Sauvage-Brown came down from the hill.

She stood glaring at him, the shotgun broken over her arm, a dumpy, scowling woman who resented his presence as an intrusion. 'You not gone in yet?'

Arnold shook his head. 'I was just looking at this.'

'The old pigsty?'

'That's it. *Very* old.'

'Rubbish.'

'True.'

Her head cocked on one side and she stared at him, summing him up. Perhaps there was something in the gravity of his tone that puzzled her, for after a moment she drew nearer and looked over the old sty, sniffing as she did so, as though odour would betray secrets not apparent to her.

'What do you mean, very old?'

Carefully Arnold said, 'Well, not all of it. The outer walls, for instance, they'll have been erected maybe a hundred years ago.'

'And that's not very old?'

'Not in relation to the roof.'

She glanced at him unbelievingly and then turned again to gaze at the rusty corrugated iron, the tiles and the lichen-covered slates.

'So what's so old about the roof?'

Arnold pointed. 'The part that's collapsed, then the repaired section, that area isn't so old. But you see those slates? By my guess they'll be maybe three hundred years old.'

There was a long, stupefied silence. When Mildred Sauvage-Brown looked at him again her heavy face was dark as though she thought he was trying to insult her intelligence. 'How in the hell can you think that?'

Arnold smiled. He raised a hand, pointed carefully. 'Look at the top edge of those slates. You see the double line of holes? These days, when slates are used on roofs they use copper nails — better than iron nails because the iron rusts.

'So?' Mildred Sauvage-Brown asked belligerently. 'Before they began to use copper nails, oak pegs were favoured. Too expensive now. But those nails holding these slates are rusted in — yet look at the smaller holes just beside them. Do you know what they once held?'

'You're going to tell me.' The Border Country accent was gone. Miss Sauvage-Brown was listening, concentrating, and a slight hint of her transatlantic tone was creeping in, even after all these years of English residence.

'The small leg bones of sheep,' Arnold said confidently.

'What the hell are you talking about?'

'Believe me. It was a common practice in the North until well after Tudor times. Sheep bones — tough and cheaper than nails. Go take a look at Walworth Castle in County Durham sometime: they used to use the breastbones of chicken there.'

Mildred Sauvage-Brown was saying something under her breath as Arnold walked away. It sounded like a string of vague obscenities.

* * *

Inside the farmhouse the air was warm with the blazing fire in the eighteenth-century fireplace. The furniture was old, the floor of the hallway and kitchen stone-flagged, and the whole atmosphere was one of utility rather than comfort. Yet the tea that was served to Arnold came from fine china and the woman who served it was small, birdlike, gentle and shy.

Sarah Ellis was no more than five feet tall and gave the impression she had been built for domination. She fluttered rather than moved, and she kept her grey head lowered, unwilling to hold Arnold's glance for more than a few seconds. Her voice was light, barely audible, and Arnold guessed that she had spent most of her sixty years attempting to escape confrontation. She wore a brown cardigan over a high-buttoned blouse, long dark skirt and flat-heeled shoes. She was nervous at his presence, yet struggled to contain her nervousness, as though she had been trained to regard politeness to guests as a duty. After Arnold had introduced himself at the gate she had invited him inside to the parlour, quickly produced a pot of tea and displayed some agitation until Mildred Sauvage-Brown had joined them. Up till then Arnold had managed only to elicit her name, the period she had spent at Penbrook Farm — fifteen years — and explain his own presence. Once her companion arrived Sarah Ellis retreated gratefully over her cup of tea to listen rather than to participate.

'So what is it you want to know from Sarah?' Mildred Sauvage-Brown growled. She had removed the woollen cap and the jacket: the grey sweater was baggy and her hair tended to stick up wilfully from the crown of her head.

'I merely thought it would be appropriate to discuss with you the proposals that are being made concerning the establishment of an old people's home at the farm, the purchase order—'

'They tell you they got plans to build over the hill?'

'I am aware of that—'

'It's all a fix, a deal they've made. Build the sop — the old folk's home — and then rake in the profits from a whole damned new village where no one but rich characters want it!'

'That's not quite the gist of their application—'

'Bet your ass it isn't!' Mildred Sauvage-Brown remarked balefully.

Arnold blinked, unused to the chameleon nature of the lady's language: the guttural Northumbrian sound had gone, and Americanisms were clearly creeping back. He wondered whether she adopted High Hampshire in planning tribunals.

'What I do wish to find out is the nature of the objections you'll wish to raise to the proposals,' he ventured.

'Objections?' Mildred Sauvage-Brown glared at Sarah Ellis. 'The first objection I'd be making on behalf of Sarah is that these bloody businessmen are seeking to turn a gentle old lady out of her home!'

'You'll be making?' Arnold asked. 'You have an interest in Penbrook Farm?'

'Interest?' To Arnold's alarm, Mildred Sauvage-Brown put down her cup, rose, walked to the fireplace, hawked and spat in the fire. 'What you really mean is do I qualify as an "aggrieved person" under your bloody ineffective planning acts. Well, I don't but Sarah sure as hell does as owner of the farm, and I'm preparing her case and I'll make damn sure she's not railroaded out of here. She's a sweet, gentle lady who's been put upon most of her life and I'm making sure it certainly don't happen this time.'

The sweet gentle lady made a gesture of feeble remonstration; it was ignored by the formidable Mildred. 'You know, I spent a few years in the south of England before I got sick of the whole attitude down there and came north. You damned English, you don't seem to know what you're doing with your heritage! Okay, the Romans didn't know better and carved a fair chunk of woodland out of the place, but by the Middle Ages woods were valuable property. It was a woodland economy, sure, and buildings were greedy for wood—'

'I understand it took six hundred and eighty oaks to build Norwich Cathedral's roof in the fifteenth century,' Arnold interrupted.

Mildred Sauvage-Brown stopped, glared at him, and opened her mouth silently. It was clear she was uncertain whether she was being mocked, and mockery of the kind that quoted supporting facts to her own obvious thesis was a ploy she had not previously met and was unable to cope with adequately. She snorted after a moment, and went on.

'In that economy, men learned to live with the woods. They managed them as a self-generating resource. They didn't clear-fell them. They raised sturdy new wood from the broad-leaved trees they'd put to the woodman's axe. Ash and horn beam were cut in rotation—'

'I'm aware—'

'Coppicing extended the life of trees: there's a coppiced ash I found in Suffolk that must have taken root a hundred years before the Conquest. They dug it out, for a public lavatory! That's when I came north!'

'Miss Sauvage-Brown, I can assure you—'

'Assure me nothing! I know you clowns. Anything for a quiet life! You planning inspectors are all the same. I shouted my head off at fifty inquiries in Hampshire and Suffolk but all they were concerned with were commuters for God's sake! So I came north, to the dales first, and then the Border Country where there was air, and hills, and a feeling of ancient times. But there are still attacks, and I've vowed I'll save you bastards from yourselves — protect the heritage you haven't the sense and guts to defend yourselves!'

'Please,' Arnold said firmly. 'I feel the same way you do. I think the heritage is important. But I'm here to discover whether there are any sound reasons you can put forward to overturn the planning application that's coming forward from Messrs Wilson and Livingstone — with a certain political backing, I might add—'

'I might have guessed *that*!'

'But it would certainly help if you were to outline the case you intend to raise,' Arnold went on. 'If there are matters I can take into account I'll be able to raise them at the inquiry, include recommendations in my report—'

'Mr Landon, we don't trust planning inspectors—'

'Mildred . . .' Sarah Ellis had raised a hand, meekly, as though to remonstrate gently with her companion, calm her down. Mildred Sauvage-Brown hesitated, then nodded, patted the older woman's hand and returned to her seat. Grumpily she said, 'All right, I can give you one matter we'll be raising.'

'That is?'

She gestured with her thumb in the direction of the hillside behind the farm. 'The woods, up there.'

'What about them?' Arnold asked.

'Not up to much for timber purposes. Oak, ash, some beech and hazel. An *old* wood, Mr Landon. A wood that's survived centuries because it grows on ground too poor to be used for anything else. But the result is there's mediaeval banks and ditches up there. And more. There's yellow archangel, bluebell, oxlip and herb Paris, all the true species of a primary woodland, slow to spread or regenerate, classic indicators of a wood that may well have existed since Domesday. And don't tell me *that* word don't stir an Englishman.'

Sarah Ellis put out a soft, heavy-veined hand to touch her companion's arm. 'Please, Mildred, don't get so excited. I'm sure Mr Landon has come here to help.'

'So what's he got to say about the ancient woodland?' Unhappily Sarah rose and drifted across to the other side of the parlour. She picked up a small dark missal and clutched it to herself as though seeking strength from it.

Arnold shook his head. 'I have to say, ladies, you'll not get much return out of that argument.'

'Why not?'

'Because the woodland you mention is not in danger. The plans cater for the retention of the woods. They'll be part of the . . . pleasing environment of the old people's home.'

Mildred Sauvage-Brown grunted triumphantly.

'Is there anything else?' Arnold asked.

'Nothing I'm prepared to discuss with you,' Mildred Sauvage-Brown snapped.

Arnold felt sad. He was aware that behind the woman's bitterness and awkwardness lay a real passion for the countryside — his countryside — but her aggressiveness made it difficult for him to explain his own feelings about the situation. He too was opposed to the Wilsons and the Livingstones of the modern world, but he was a planning officer and he had his duty to do. As Sarah Ellis, the ineffectual owner of Penbrook Farm, fluttered in the background, he rose and took his leave of the two ladies.

Mildred Sauvage-Brown followed him out as though she feared he would indulge in minor despoliations as he left. She stood staring at him thoughtfully as he unlocked his car, arms folded muscularly across her ample bosom and then, as he got in behind the driving wheel, she suddenly came across to him.

'When I was talking back there, doing my usual niggle about what you planning bastards have done to the countryside you gave me a brief impression—'

'Yes?'

'That maybe you . . . cared,' Mildred Sauvage-Brown said unwillingly.

'I do.'

'Why?'

'Do I need a reason?'

'Don't play games with me, mister.'

'I'm not playing games,' Arnold said seriously. 'Look, I've got a job to do. That doesn't mean I'm not . . . sympathetic. I think some of your . . . aggression can cause damage to your case but that's up to you. But I was brought up in the Yorkshire Dales by a father who was a craftsman, and he's passed on to me a lot of his knowledge and a lot of his love for wood, and stone. So I do understand. And I do care.'

'Enough to help?'

Arnold hesitated. 'It depends what you mean by help.'

Mildred Sauvage-Brown glowered, then jerked a beefy thumb over her shoulder. 'That pigsty.'

'Yes?'

'You say it's old . . . awful old.'

'Part of it is.'

'You can prove that?'

'If I were called to do so.'

She turned and inspected the slated roof from a distance. 'Those slates . . . whatever you say, they don't look so old to me. Clean, like they was almost machined.'

Arnold leaned out of the window. He shook his head. 'The old slaters, they used the best tool of all. Frost.'

'*Frost*?'

'That stone is laminated oolite. What you had to do was quarry it in the autumn, lay the slabs of stone on the ground and then water them every evening from December through to March, if necessary.'

'What the hell for?'

'It was essential the stone remained green — if the quarry sap dried out of the slabs the stone could be used only for dry walling, or road metalling, or burned for quicklime.'

'And the frost?'

'The force of even a single thaw, following a hard frost, could achieve in a few hours what it could take a man weeks to do. It would crack the stone into clean, flat layers of varying thickness. After that, the slater would just cleave the stone along the fissures and trim each piece with a hammer.'

'Then hole the slate near the head,' the woman said thoughtfully.

'That's right, so it could be fixed to a batten.'

'With an oak peg, the leg bone of a sheep,' Mildred Sauvage-Brown said with a gleam in her eye, 'or even a measly little chicken bone.'

'Oh dear,' Arnold said to himself as he started the car, put it in gear and drove bumpily up over the hill and away from Penbrook Farm. The Senior Planning Officer wasn't going to like this: he wasn't going to like it one little bit.

CHAPTER TWO

1

The fact that the Senior Planning Officer was leaving for his holiday in Scarborough in a few days meant that Arnold was not called upon to explain about Penbrook Farm when he returned to his office in Morpeth. A natural preoccupation with his intended east coast sojourn resulted in the Senior Planning Officer having little regard for anything still lying on his desk during those last few days before he escorted his wife southwards. They were travelling by train. His wife distrusted his driving skills.

It was an occasion, therefore, when Arnold was able to relax somewhat and not feel concerned that the files he was dealing with were likely at any moment to be whisked away and scrawled upon with a spidery hand; when discussions with architects were in no danger of interruption by a demand to be 'briefed'; and when Arnold could feel clear of the necessity to sit for an hour or more while the Senior Planning Officer commented upon his wife's inferior cooking and his resentment at Arnold's failure to take to himself a similarly happy marital situation.

It meant Arnold was left more to his own devices, of course, and was free within certain limits to make his own decisions without fear of being countermanded immediately, but this was not a situation he entirely relished: he was not an ambitious man and had no desire for the acquisition of the power wielded by the Senior Planning Officer. Nor did he wish to be privileged by visits from councillors, wishing to talk to the man in charge.

When councillors did come into his office, it was usually by mistake. It was Arnold's habit to direct them quickly to the office along the corridor. He did so that afternoon, when the man in the neat grey suit entered his office.

'You'll want the Senior Planning Officer. Just along the corridor.'

The man nodded, turned, then stopped at the door. He glanced back thoughtfully at Arnold. He was perhaps six feet tall, with a whipcord leanness to his body and a thin, narrow face in which the eyes gleamed watchfully. He was about forty years old, perhaps a little more.

'You're Landon, aren't you?'

'That's right. Mr . . . ?'

'My name's Minford.' Councillor Minford. A youngish man to have been so active in local politics during the last ten years or so since his father's death and the closing down of the family business. That Albert Minford was no pauper as a result of the closure was evident from his dress: his shirt was expensive, his shoes soft, rich leather. He moved quietly, almost catlike in grace, and he made Arnold feel uneasy at the insistence in his glance. It was full of calculation and summaries, a polishing of opinions.

'We've not met before,' Minford said.

'That's right. I've heard of you, of course, Councillor.'

'And I of you, Mr Landon.' It was a casual statement, and contained no obvious weight, yet Arnold felt his spine prickle uneasily. 'You have obtained a reputation for certain unusual . . . involvements during this last year or so.'

'My job—'

'Oh, no criticism of your work. Unusual interests, though. I like that.' His eyes said otherwise: they betrayed no real interest. 'Keeps a man . . . balanced, having other interests. I . . . ah . . . understand the Senior Planning Officer takes leave soon.'

'For a couple of weeks.'

'You'll be working at the planning hearing for Penbrook Farm.'

'I will.'

'You'll have reached conclusions.'

They were not questions, but statements, delivered in a flat, unemotional and yet oddly menacing tone. Arnold blinked, unsure of himself. 'I suppose you could say that.'

'And?'

Arnold hesitated, then shrugged. 'I'm not sure what you want to know, Councillor. I've been out to the farm, had a look around. I've read the papers prepared by the petitioners.'

'They have council support.'

'That's right.'

'So it should be straightforward.'

Reluctantly, Arnold nodded. He had in his mind a glimpse of a belligerent Mildred Sauvage-Brown, but he kept the image to himself. Albert Minford's eyes bored into him. Arnold waited.

At last, with a vaguely dissatisfied air, Councillor Minford turned away. At the door he paused, looked back towards Arnold thoughtfully and said, 'You've been with the department quite a while, Mr Landon.'

'Quite a while, Councillor.'

'Loyalty . . . to the department gets rewarded.'

Arnold said nothing. Albert Minford let the silence between them deepen. He had said nothing that was dangerous, made no commitment by way of an offer, and yet there lay between them something unspoken, a gift dangling, a reward to be grasped if only Arnold cared to stretch out his hand. Slowly, Minford nodded and left the room. He closed the door softly behind him. He would do everything softly, Arnold fancied, until he was crossed. Then the softness could well become merely the sheath for steel.

He sighed. It was all very well, the Senior Planning Officer going off like this, but it meant that Arnold was really snowed under with work. There was the Willington Hall file as well as Penbrook Farm. The Willington Hall application would have to be dealt with within the week at the same time as Penbrook was pending. And then there was the new application regarding Amble. Complicated — a new company, a development that was almost bound to raise objections, but something that the town itself might welcome in general to halt its gradual decline over the years.

And it would require a visit.

Arnold left the office at two in the afternoon. It was a bright day, and the early morning frost had disappeared from the roads although the hills towards the Cheviot were white-summited, sparkling in the bright air. Arnold drove north from Morpeth, taking the bypass towards Alnwick. Then, where the road dipped towards the ancient bridge at Felton, he turned right and meandered along the winding road that led to the coast. Furrowed fields to his left glistened with frost and high above the hedgerow a sparrowhawk hovered, wings hardly quivering in the afternoon sun.

Warkworth Castle stood on the hillside overlooking the village, its ruined windows staring blankly downriver towards Amble. Arnold parked in the main street and walked back up the road towards the castle, crossed the moated bridge and entered the castle grounds. There was no keeper at the gate: tourists arrived only in the summer months and today there was no charge for entry. Arnold climbed the well-preserved walls and stood in the embrasure, looking out to the sea.

The breeze was keen at this height and he hunched in his overcoat. Below him the town lay warm in the hollow of the hill; the river crept in a slow half-circle around the town, under the old bridge where the martins nested, and then snaked seawards in a long, glittering coil. Two miles away he could see the first of the masted fishing boats. They lay drawn up at the river edge, high and dry: when the tide came upstream, flooding the bar at Warkworth itself, they would ride gently on the swell. Beyond, as the river widened, the houses at Amble clustered at the bay. Church, warehouses, dark, decaying buildings of the waterfront. Arnold stared, and considered. A development there . . . it could pump summer life into Amble, even if winter would still be cold in the empty town.

Thoughtfully he made his way back to the high street.

* * *

He had parked on the steep hill above the market cross. A line of shops and offices ran opposite him and in one of the office doorways a man was standing. As Arnold began to unlock his car door the man raised his hand and walked across the street towards him.

'Arnold! What are you doing in Warkworth?'

Arnold Landon did not make friends easily. He lived alone and liked it, and his own personal interests tended to isolate him somewhat: few people were interested in discussing ancient wood and stone. His weekends were spent wandering in the villages and hills of Northumberland and Cumbria, seeking and identifying traces of lost worlds, mediaeval, Norman, Saxon, Roman. Opportunities for social intercourse were few.

He did not exactly count Freddie Keeler as a friend, but the man's outgoing personality made it easy to talk to him when they met, and Keeler's own effusiveness was warming. He was an estate agent and auctioneer whom Arnold had met some years earlier when he was working in the Town Clerk's department. They had met from time to time in Morpeth and for some curious reason Keeler had taken Arnold under his wing socially, inviting him for a lunchtime drink occasionally on Saturdays, when they had met in town. Arnold hesitated now, and smiled lopsidedly.

'I might ask you the same,' he replied.

Freddie Keeler grinned, stopped, struck a pose and made a theatrical gesture back towards the doorway he had left.

'Expanding!' he declaimed. 'Opened an office in Warkworth, haven't I?'

Keeler and Buckley. The sign was there; Arnold hadn't noticed it.

'I thought you worked Northumberland from the Morpeth office,' Arnold said.

'Ah yes, but it's all a matter of confidence. You won't realize it, but there's a hell of a lot of auction stuff goes begging up here in the hinterland. Large houses, old folks, they sell up and the sharks come up from London and Manchester, but they don't like dealing with them. They like a local dealer — someone they feel they can trust. And that means you gotta be there, boy! Here, that is, if you want to catch the stuff in the Border Country. Might even have to set a place going in Jedburgh, eventually.'

Arnold nodded, smiling at Keeler's enthusiasm. He was a tubby little man in his fifties, with sparse hair, a rolling gait he claimed to have developed on the Tyne ferry as a young man, and broad, red-knuckled hands. He wore a tweed jacket and cavalry twill trousers as though he had just discovered the fashion: there was something dated about him, but it was an endearing quality. 'I've come up to take a look at Amble,' Arnold explained.

'Amble?' Keeler knitted his brows. 'Planning business? Oh yeah, wait a minute, didn't I see something in the local rag?'

'It's possible.'

Keeler scratched his nose, glanced back over his shoulder and said, 'Tell you what, nothing much happening in the office, got a girl there anyway, I'll come down with you for a trip, hey? You can easily come back this way on the return, can't you? No need to go straight back to Morpeth. Might even be time for a swift half, if we wait till opening time!'

There seemed little Arnold could say by way of argument. Feebly he suggested Keeler might get a rush of business while he was away but the estate agent brushed the argument aside and clambered in beside Arnold. Together they drove down the river road towards Amble, leaving Warkworth at their backs.

Arnold had never liked the town particularly. It had grown rapidly in Victorian times with the growth of the fishing industry and the building of the coal staithes on the shoreline. The disappearance of the brigs hauling coal south, and the decline of first the coal and then the fishing industry had left the urban sprawl of red brick terraces without a reason for existence. The town centre had decayed and the shoreline itself had become a wasteland, the gaunt ribs of the old wooden gantries and coal staithes leaning with the sea gales against empty expanses of shale and coal slurry. A hundred years ago barges and brigs, proud-masted and heavy with cargo, had moored alongside the pier head, but the pier itself was now a rickety affair, planking and guard-rails ravaged by wind and rain and exhaustion. Part of it had been fenced off with chicken wire in an ineffectual warning ignored by schoolchildren; the staggering steps that were available alongside were still in use for the few pleasure boats that came alongside, and for the school training vessels that skirted the moonscaped land to brave the bar and the North Sea beyond.

Arnold stood alongside Freddie Keeler above the wooden railings. They stared out towards the bar and the white foam boiled in its surge as the wind shifted.

'Do you reckon they'll make a go of it?' Freddie Keeler asked.

'Of what?'

'The proposed marina.'

Arnold shrugged. 'I've no idea. I just look at these things in terms of planning applications. Whether they'll make it pay, that's another matter.'

'Local opinion says the whole scheme is farcical, Keeler said. 'I mean, look at the coastline. Best beaches in the country, but empty because of inaccessibility and the damned wind that scours the sands on even the sunniest days. Fine harbours, but developed for a fishing industry that's all but disappeared. So who's going to come up here and start a yachting club? I mean, take the moors: shotguns are in plentiful supply along the rough shoots above Stanley to County Durham and landowners from that moor right up through the length of Northumberland have made a packet by playing the market, raising grouse and pheasant, drawing in London businessmen and Saudi potentates. I mean, damn it, there's all sorts of languages talked along the fells these days!'

'So I understand.'

Freddie Keeler wrinkled his nose, shrugged, and shoved his hands deep into the pockets of his overcoat. 'Saudis tired of hawking are one thing; can you imagine dhows racing on the Coquet? I tell you, man, the whole thing is crazy!'

'Is that the opinion of the press?'

'There was a leader in the *Gazette* just the other day, Arnold. Said the scheme was a load of nonsense. To talk of boats returning to Amble is a pipe dream. There'll never be a return, hinny — no more than the coal will come back. What would be the point of mooring here at Amble, to this wasteland? Good harbour, sure, but there's facilities just up river towards Warkworth. The castle to set the scene, a couple of decent pubs . . . who'd want to moor down here, with the wind whistling in from the North Sea straight up your backside?'

'Facilities could be improved,' Arnold suggested cautiously.

'So the Geordie Coast will compete with the Cote d'Azur?' Keeler scoffed. 'It's all a con, man, building a marina here. Waste of money. Unless . . .'

'Yes?'

'Unless it's someone else's money. Like yours and mine.'

Public money. It was a possibility that had already occurred to Arnold.

2

A week later the planning inquiry into the application regarding Penbrook Farm was convened at Morpeth. Wilson and Livingstone both arrived at the council chamber early, and Arnold was interested to note that they regarded the inquiry as an important one, since they had engaged the services of counsel to speak on their behalf and introduce the application.

Arnold knew the man they had engaged: Arthur Sedleigh-Harmon, QC. He was a Chancery lawyer with a big London practice but a Northern circuit background, which enabled him to make forays north from time to time. It was hinted that he was a mean man, who undertook such briefs in order to be able, at his clients' expense, to indulge his passion, fly-fishing in the Border Country. Arnold had always thought him incapable of any passion: he was a tall, round-shouldered, dry stick of a man, hook-nosed, glazed-eyed, with a neat, trimmed moustache and a flat monotonous voice. But he was a successful lawyer, sharp-minded and incisive in his questions. He understood a witness's balance, or lack of it: he could topple a case with a question.

Mildred Sauvage-Brown was also in the council chamber, accompanying Sarah Ellis. Miss Ellis was dressed in self-effacing brown; Mildred Sauvage-Brown, on the other hand, had discarded her woollen cap, tweed jacket and black skirt, and had dressed for the occasion in a heavy, mannish suit, belted at the waist, and a feathered Robin Hood hat was perched incongruously on her untidy grey curls. She had applied a red bow of lipstick to her mouth; it contrasted with powdered cheeks from which glared angry eyes, as though she dared mockery. Her glance slipped over Arnold dismissively. She watched Arthur Sedleigh-Harmon like a mongoose watching a snake.

The Queen's Counsel introduced the application in his flat monotone. Chairman of the planning committee was an elderly gentleman called Lansbury who claimed distant kin to the Labour politician of a bygone era; he was known to be ineffectual and inclined to doze. Sedleigh-Harmon's voice was conducive to an exaggeration of his inclination.

The application, Sedleigh-Harmon droned, would be one from which considerable benefit would accrue to the community, not least the elderly and infirm. The Twilight Home would be what it implied in its title: a haven for the old in which they would see out their days in quiet and comfort.

Mildred Sauvage-Brown snorted.

The monotone continued. Details of the layout of the home together with its configuration were appended in the schedule to the application; there would be minimal damage to the environment; service and access roads would be located in a fold in the land so as to cause the minimum disruption of the peace of the area. . .

Mildred Sauvage-Brown snorted again, and Sarah Ellis placed a timid hand on her companion's arm. Chairman Lansbury's eyelids grew heavy.

'And with that, Chairman, I will take my seat, although I am happy to take any queries at this stage,' Sedleigh-Harmon announced abruptly, and sat down.

Startled, Lansbury sat up, sniffing and scratching his cheeks in a sudden panic, until he remembered where he was and the purpose of the inquiry. An official at his elbow whispered to him. He coughed, cleared his throat. 'Ah . . . I understand there are objections to the proposals. Perhaps we could have a submission at this point?'

Formidably, Mildred Sauvage-Brown rose to her feet.

Chairman Lansbury looked vaguely unhappy: clearly, he had met the lady at earlier hearings.

'Ah, Miss Sauvage-Brown. You are objecting to the application?'

'On behalf of the owner, Miss Sarah Ellis. We,' she intoned, sweeping a contemptuous glance over the group sitting across the room and comprising Wilson, Livingstone and Sedleigh-Harmon, 'cannot afford the services of eminent counsel.'

Arnold settled back. There was a nervous feeling in his stomach. Mildred Sauvage-Brown was not the kind of person to give up anything without a fight, and he had a feeling he was likely to end up right in the middle of her battlefield. It was not a prospect he viewed with any feeling of enjoyment.

'Chairman, in the beginning was the wildwood, the home of the wolf and brown bear,' Mildred Sauvage-Brown boomed. 'Even in the Stone Age three men with axes could fell an acre of forest in a morning — stone axes, Chairman! When the Celtic tribes arrived with iron tools and ploughs the rate of attrition was greater still. The Romans—'

'Chairman, may I interrupt?' Sedleigh-Harmon was rising to his feet, a bored expression on his hatchet features. 'The history of the wildwood in Britain is of no consequence to this hearing. Miss Sauvage-Brown is going to refer to an ancient woodland on the property, but the redevelopment of Penbrook Farm will not affect . . . this woodland, so we really do not need to waste time on this discourse.'

Mildred Sauvage-Brown expanded her formidable bosom. 'Waste time! When the heritage of England is being systematically destroyed by vandals like you! I insist—'

Chairman Lansbury raised sufficient nerve to lift a restraining hand. 'Please, Miss Sauvage-Brown, a moment.' When, reluctantly, she subsided, he turned to look at Arnold.

'Mr Landon, as planning officer involved you have studied this application?'

'Yes, Chairman,' Arnold replied, half-rising.

'Do you have any comment?'

'The development, as learned counsel suggests, does not affect the ancient woodlands on the hill, to which reference is probably being made.'

'Thank you.' The Chairman glanced nervously towards Miss Sauvage-Brown. 'No more wildwood, please. Will you continue?'

Mildred Sauvage-Brown ignored him for several seconds. Instead, she directed her glance towards Arnold. It was a compound of contempt and hatred: he should have been supporting her in her fight, but he was a craven coward. Arnold moved, wriggling uncomfortably in his seat. Satisfied, Mildred Sauvage-Brown returned to her task.

'Under protest, Chairman, I will say no more about the woodland, nor about the mediaeval ditches and the coppices which mark it. I will say nothing about the deprivations of years; I will make no comment upon the damaging attitudes which have brought such woodlands to their knees, or the methods landowners have used to milk the tax system. I will say no more on these matters, important though they are, and even though I am far from certain that once this development is approved that woodland would not be at risk as a result of further depredations. No,' she cried triumphantly, 'I will draw attention to another matter entirely.' And she leaned forward, groped underneath her seat and raised aloft a rolled sheet of paper. 'Can I have a demonstration stand, Chairman?'

A rumbling consternation followed with the Chairman, wide awake, concerned to provide via his ushers an appropriate stand on which the objector, in the form of Mildred Sauvage-Brown, could obtain an adequate demonstration of her case. He wanted no appeal to a tribunal on the grounds of failure of natural justice, *audi alteram partem*, or any such nonsense. After several minutes' delay a sheepish county officer came in with the advice that the only item available was a blackboard.

It was brought in, without ceremony. It stood to one side of the council chamber while the formidable Miss Sauvage-Brown, who had had the foresight to arm herself in advance with a suitable number of drawing pins, proceeded to tack her rolled sheet of paper to the board.

It consisted of a neatly drawn sketch. As Mildred Sauvage-Brown began to explain, Arnold leaned forward, craning to read the legend on the sketch-map. *Penbrook Farm: where time stood still.*

As she spoke, he inspected the sketch.

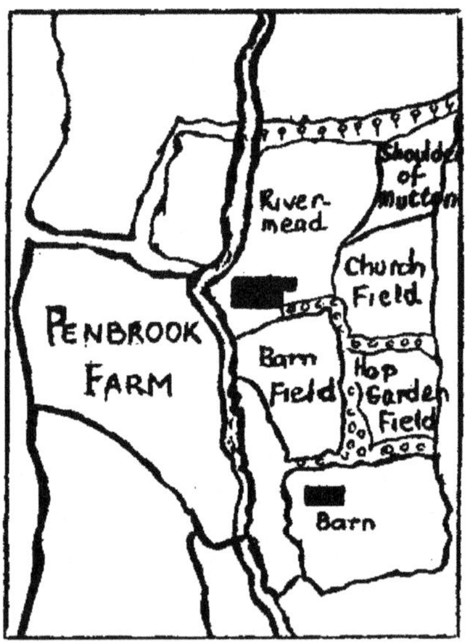

'One of the contentions in the planning application made by Mr Wilson and Mr Livingstone, and so *ably*,' she sneered, 'presented by eminent counsel, is that Penbrook Farm is not a going concern. I think the owner, my friend Sarah Ellis, for whom I am speaking, would agree. The farm itself cannot be seen as a profit-making business.'

She waved a hand towards the sketch, taking in the boundaries. 'The thirty acres or so that you see here provide little more than a modest hay crop, and perhaps enough winter grazing for a handful of sheep. But Sarah Ellis knew that when she bought Penbrook Farm fifteen years ago. It was never her intention to make it a 'going concern'. She came to it, fell in love with it, bought it, for reasons far divorced from the money-grubbing motivations of the Wilsons and the Livingstones of this world. The fact is, Chairman, the value of Penbrook Farm to naturalists is incalculable.'

'Naturalists?' the Chairman repeated doubtfully.

'Penbrook Farm,' Mildred Sauvage-Brown asserted, 'is that rare survivor in the intensively-managed countryside of the nineteen-eighties: a mediaeval farm.'

'I don't understand,' the Chairman said, but the interest in Arnold's veins quickened as he inspected the sketch on the blackboard more closely.

'Let me explain,' Mildred Sauvage-Brown boomed confidently. 'Penbrook Farm is a mediaeval farm with all its original fields, ponds and hedges intact. The farmhouse itself was pulled down in the eighteen-nineties and has been rebuilt, but the fifteenth-century barn still stands intact and I can tell you nothing much else has changed — even to the old pollards that established the woodland boundaries.'

'I don't see—'

'When farming was mechanized a hundred years ago and fields were enlarged for the new machines, Penbrook was saved because it was too small. Later, when new machines might have solved that problem, the property was bought by a man who was more interested in its possibilities as a rough shoot. As a consequence, it was still in a virginal state when bought by my friend Miss Ellis.'

'Mr Chairman,' Arthur Sedleigh-Harmon, QC, intoned, rising to his feet. 'All very interesting and . . . ah . . . emotional, but what has it to do with this inquiry? A mediaeval farm?'

Mildred Sauvage-Brown bristled and the feather in her Robin Hood hat danced furiously. 'You clearly don't appreciate the situation as a townsman . . . and a Londoner to boot! What we have at Penbrook is near to being unique! What Sarah Ellis bought fifteen years ago was a botanist's dream: Penbrook must be the largest surviving group of old flower-rich hay meadows in the north of England. Each of the fields is filled with the kinds of plants that have all but vanished elsewhere in the north—'

'Really, Chairman, I must ask for a ruling,' Sedleigh-Harmon protested.

'-yellow hay rattle, adder's tongue ferns—'

'Chairman!'

'—fantastic green winged orchids, so many wild orchids you could hardly walk without treading on them—'

'*Chairman*' Sedleigh-Harmon insisted.

Mr Lansbury, pink-cheeked, banged his fist on the table. 'Will you just stop a moment, Miss Sauvage-Brown? What point is it you're trying to make?'

Mildred Sauvage-Brown stared at him, open-mouthed, as though she could hardly believe the question was directed towards her. 'Point? *Point*? Bloody hell, man, the point is if you let this development go forward you'll be destroying something it's taken seven centuries and maybe more to establish!'

Arnold knew it was always going to be an argument that would not hold water with Mr Lansbury. There were many reasons why planning applications were thrown out by the county council, but botany was not one of them. There was no doubt that the opinions held by Miss Sauvage-Brown were sincerely and worthily held, but the opinion of Chairman Lansbury was always going to be that modern progress should not be held back or stultified by amateur botanists chasing around fields with butterfly nets or grubbing tools.

'If that,' the Chairman said firmly when Miss Sauvage-Brown had protested at length, 'is the only objection you have to raise, I think we can bring this inquiry to a swift end.'

For a long moment Mildred Sauvage-Brown glared at him, then slowly, inevitably, she turned her head. She stared almost malevolently at Arnold Landon and he felt the courage drain slowly from his veins.

'No,' she said slowly and distinctly, 'it isn't the only objection I wish to raise. With your permission, I'd like to ask some questions of the planning officer, Mr Arnold Landon.'

The Senior Planning Officer would have been *far* from pleased.

3

Standing at his seat, Arnold felt completely exposed, naked and isolated. He was accustomed to giving evidence or making statements at hearings; he never enjoyed this kind of limelight but he had grown accustomed to it. On this occasion it was different, however: he felt forebodings that weakened his knees and made him unable to meet the fierce, demanding glance of Miss Mildred Sauvage-Brown.

'The old wildwood is gone forever,' she said in a high penetrating voice. 'But would you agree that what remains is precious?'

Arnold moistened his lips with his tongue. 'I would say so, yes.'

'What does remain? A scattered mosaic of clumps and coppices, silent spinneys, lonely fox roosts, a few beech hangers, pagan groves of oak and yew—'

'Chairman, do we have to go through this again?' Sedleigh-Harmon protested flatly.

'—pocket woodlands where bluebells almost anaesthetize the senses, the miraculous depths of old, true forests—'

'*Mr Chairman*!'

Mr Lansbury banged his fist on the table in desperation. 'We've been through all this, Miss Sauvage-Brown.

You said you wanted to ask the planning officer some questions. Will you do that, instead of eulogizing the vanished countryside?'

'So what of the works of man?' Mildred Sauvage-Brown snapped.

Silence fell in the council chamber. Arnold blinked, not certain whether a question had been directed at him or at the Chairman. Mr Lansbury also seemed somewhat taken aback.

'Miss Sauvage-Brown—'

'What of the works of man?' she repeated, stabbing a chunky finger in the air, in the general direction of Arnold Landon.

'I . . . I'm not quite certain what you mean,' he prevaricated, knowing perfectly well what she meant.

She glared at him and then moved to the attack. 'Tell me, Mr Landon, what were ancient roofs made of?'

'Obviously, wood, or thatch.'

'Stone?'

'Depends how far back you go,' Arnold replied cautiously. 'Stone as a material for roofing was still pretty rare, even in the Cotswolds, up to the thirteenth century.'

'But afterwards?'

Arnold swallowed hard. 'From the fourteenth century on, primarily to avoid the risk of fire, stone began to be used as a roofing material for churches and other public buildings.'

'And private houses?'

'And private houses. Indeed, from early Tudor times,' Arnold continued, almost forgetting the pressure of the questioning, 'stone became a favourite roofing material in Sussex, Surrey, the Cotswolds, the Welsh border counties—'

'And in the North?'

'Large parts of the northern counties, from Derbyshire to Northumberland.'

'You say stone,' Miss Sauvage-Brown said cunningly, 'but the layman would speak of *slate*?'

Inwardly Arnold groaned. 'That's right. Slate.'

'Tell us about this slate.'

Arnold told them. It was odd: even Sedleigh-Harmon, QC, who had seemed on the point of interruption several times now subsided as Arnold spoke to them of the slater's craft. He told the hearing of the sandstones and the oolites, of the splitting of laminated stone, and of the trimming into the approximate sizes, with their Lewis Carroll-sounding names: *muffities* and *wivetts*, *tants* and *cussems*. 'Very often no attempt was made to produce slates of uniform size and thickness — it's been said that in the north no two slates were ever identical anyway.'

Arnold paused; the room was silent. There was a glazed look in Sedleigh-Harmon's eyes but in the stocky bearing of Mildred Sauvage-Brown there was triumph.

'All right, Mr Landon, now let me hear you tell the Chairman here what it is you found when you visited Penbrook Farm the other week!'

'I . . .' Arnold hesitated, glancing at the Queen's Counsel, at Wilson, Livingstone and beyond them the triumphant Mildred, and there was a cold feeling in his stomach. 'I found . . . I found some roofing slates that are probably at least three hundred years old.'

'And that,' Mildred Sauvage-Brown almost shouted, 'is on the farm you want to tear apart for an old people's home!'

She sat down, abruptly, as though her case was made.

There was an air of puzzlement and uncertainty in the council chamber, a vague rustling of voices as consideration was given to what Mildred Sauvage-Brown seemed to be saying. Destroy an ancient woodland; destroy a mediaeval farm; destroy a three-hundred-year-old building-it was desecration.

Arthur Sedleigh-Harmon rose slowly to his feet. He stared at Arnold as though he were awakening from a long sleep, hooded eyes blinking, the suspicion of a yawn on his mouth. 'Mr . . . er . . . Landon. Planning officer?'

'That's right.'

'You visited the farm?'

Arnold nodded, undeceived by the passivity of the tone. 'Yes.'

'And found these . . . inestimable, three-hundred-year-old slates?'

'Yes, sir.'

'Where?'

'I beg your pardon?'

'The question was clearly phrased. Where did you find the slates?'

'On . . .' The words died in Arnold's mouth, and he glanced sorrowfully towards Mildred Sauvage-Brown. 'On a pigsty.'

There was a long, ominous silence. Arthur Sedleigh-Harmon traversed the courtroom with a slow, contemptuous, incredulous glance. At length it fastened on Arnold. 'A *pigsty*?'

'Yes, sir.'

'You *must* be joking!'

'No, sir.'

'Were our ancestors accustomed, then, to using expensive *slate* to roof so humble a dwelling as a . . . *pigsty*?'

Someone in the council chamber laughed and anger touched Arnold's veins. 'Slate, Mr Sedleigh-Harmon, and three-hundred-year-old slate! Yes, our ancestors *did* use slate to roof humble dwellings! You can't go by modern ideas. There was a time, three hundred years ago, when every cottage, barn *and* pigsty had a slate roof — all were accorded the dignity of stone because they were important buildings. All right, the reverse is true nowadays: an old roof needs repair, the slates are stripped off and sold and replaced with tiles — often too red to blend — asbestos, corrugated iron, real misfortunes for a stone-built village. But even now the production of stone slates has not entirely ceased and—'

'Yes, yes,' Sedleigh-Harmon interrupted testily. He was annoyed; he realized he had made a mistake. He changed his tack, subtly, aware of a tide of sympathy that had welled up in the council chamber for days gone by, and he asked, 'How do you know the tiles . . . sorry, *slates*, are that old?'

'The peg holes — they are unique to the North.'

'How?'

'Size. They weren't made for the normal oak pegs or nails. They are much smaller.'

'So what kind of pegs were used?' Sedleigh-Harmon asked, carefully, his instinct telling him he was near something of importance.

'Bones, sir. Sheep . . . or chicken.'

'Well, well, well . . .' Sedleigh-Harmon expressed his astonishment flatly and stared at Arnold, one hand creeping up to caress the thin, pencil moustache he affected. 'You can, then, vouch for the age of these slates?'

'Yes, sir.'

'How?'

Arnold's heart sank. 'Because I've seen others like them.'

'In the North?'

'Yes, sir.'

'*Where*!' The question came like a snake striking.

'Walworth Castle, sir. Winchcombe Manor. Dene House—'

'How many examples can you name, say, in Durham and Northumberland?' Sedleigh-Harmon asked silkily.

Arnold hesitated. 'Perhaps . . . perhaps a dozen.'

'All in stately homes?'

Arnold shook his head dumbly. He was aware of the powerful form of Mildred Sauvage-Brown shaking with anger across to his left. 'No, sir.'

'Let me get the picture clearly then, Mr Landon. You aver there are ancient slates . . . on an ancient pigsty at Penbrook Farm. But these slates, and their . . . ah . . . location, are by no means unique in the North-East? There are several other, similar examples . . . ?'

'That is so.'

'It follows, does it not, that if the development of Penbrook Farm were to go ahead, over the objections of Miss Sarah Ellis and her able companion Miss Mildred Sauvage-Brown, and this . . . *pigsty* were to be destroyed, there would be no great loss to anyone, other than, perhaps . . . future generations of pigs?'

As laughter rippled around the council chamber Arnold inclined his head miserably. He had been dreading this moment for some time; he had known that Mildred Sauvage-Brown would have had expectations he had foolishly, raised. He had hoped she would not have raised the issue, hoped desperately he would not be called upon to support her . . . and then fail her. 'There are . . . other examples,' he said. 'The pigsty at Penbrook Farm is not unique.'

And to his horror, Mildred Sauvage-Brown stood up in the council chamber and shouted wildly at him shaking her fist. 'Traitor! You know that, Landon? You're a bloody traitor!'

4

The words echoed painfully in Arnold's mind for the rest of the day. It was not as though they had been unexpected: he had known from the moment he'd told Mildred Sauvage-Brown about the old slates on the pigsty that it was likely she'd use the information to try to oppose the development. Equally, he had always known it would be an attempt doomed to frustration in that he would not have been able in all conscience, to agree the find was of sufficient importance to support her case. She had seen him as a traitor — to her, to Sarah Ellis and to conservationists the length of England. But it had been inevitable.

The inevitability did not make it easier. He had felt great sympathy for her stand. He disliked her personally: she was the kind of upper class, meddling, aggressive personality he had no time for and instinctively distrusted, but he still understood and appreciated the cause she was standing for and fighting for. He wished he could have helped her more than he did, but it was not possible, not on the grounds she had wanted to use.

The scene had worsened, of course. Once she knew he would not be able to support her she had turned vicious, screamed at him in the courtroom, throwing off the restraining arm of her timid friend, and then she had turned her wrath on her real enemies, Wilson and Livingstone. It had brought a quick end to the hearing, with the Chairman deeming all objections answered. He had beat a hasty retreat, with Mr Sedleigh-Harmon, QC, uttering dire warnings that if Miss Mildred Sauvage-Brown did not desist in her scandalous and scurrilous remarks he would be advising his clients to take action for defamation.

Yet the words she had used and the claims she had made had bothered Arnold. It was unlikely there was anything in what she had said, but nevertheless he felt it was something he should be looking into. He would have done so, that afternoon, had he not had a visitor to his office.

Henry Willington had arrived unannounced. He tapped on the door, opened it and entered with a certain diffidence. 'Have you recovered somewhat now, Mr Landon?'

For a moment Arnold had been puzzled. Then, still sweating, he shook his head wryly. 'You saw the scene in the corridor.'

'I saw you coming out of the council chamber,' Willington remarked, 'all but pursued by that harridan. You'll forgive me for saying so, Mr Landon, but you shouldn't tangle with determined ladies twice your size!'

Arnold smiled, in spite of himself. 'She was somewhat . . . upset. I had been unable to support her in the planning inquiry and she wanted to vent her anger upon me.'

'It'll cost you — or her — a new shirt,' Willington said, gesturing towards Arnold's torn collar.

Arnold shook his head. 'She was . . . distraught. And in a way it was partly my own fault. A determined and forceful lady . . . and accustomed to demonstrating her point of view.

'There wasn't much point in the other lady trying to stop her either. She was hanging on grimly, but it was like trying to hang on to a hurricane.'

'Miss Ellis. She actually owns Penbrook Farm. Mildred Sauvage-Brown is her companion. I think she was hugely embarrassed by the whole scene, but the fact is it was all being done for Miss Ellis's benefit, so I suppose she felt duty bound to save Miss Sauvage-Brown from the excesses of her own temper.'

'As you say, a very forceful lady. Companion to Miss Ellis . . .' Henry Willington frowned, and sat down near the door. He contemplated his hands for a few moments, still frowning, and then he said, 'I hope you don't mind me calling in like this, without an appointment.'

'The afternoon's almost over.' Arnold looked at the young man's bent head. The fair hair was thin on the crown, pink skin showing beneath. He was gripping his hands together tightly, as though concerned about something, holding tight rein on himself. 'I've no other appointments,' Arnold added.

'I was in town,' Willington said. He raised his head, his pale brown eyes cold. 'I thought I'd take the chance to call in, have a chat with you about that damned plan of my father's.'

'I'm available, Mr Willington.'

Henry Willington frowned. 'Is there any way I can quietly withdraw the application?'

'Your father is the owner of Willington Hall,' Arnold replied. 'You're his heir?'

'For what it's worth,' Willington replied bitterly. 'There'll be little enough left of the *patrimony* as it is; if the old man gets this application through and sinks more money into, it . . . damn it, Mr Landon, you know the scheme is crazy!'

Arnold nodded. 'In my consideration it will be a waste of money. But the planning committee are unlikely to turn it down merely on that account. Patrick Willington may be a poor businessman, but that is of no account to them.

'It's of damn serious account to me,' Henry Willington exclaimed with a flash of impatience. 'He's all but ruined the estate, what's left of it, and this bloody stupid scheme . . . He's a sick man, Mr Landon.'

Something cold touched Arnold's spine. Carefully he said, 'I saw no evidence of . . . sickness.'

'I could get him certified,' Henry Willington said and his pale eyes were cold.

'I don't think that's an area into which I could stray,' Arnold said hurriedly. 'As for the scheme—'

'He had a bit of a turn the other day,' Willington added, almost to himself. 'I wanted to call the doctor then, but the old fool wouldn't let me. One of these days . . . Anyway, you think there's little chance the committee will throw out the scheme?'

'I can't say. It will partly depend upon what objections may be raised to it. Will . . . er . . . will you be making any objections?'

'To my father's pet scheme to turn around the Willington fortunes?' Henry Willington's smile was bitter. 'No, I couldn't do that.' He stood up suddenly. 'A setback, some opposition like that . . . I mean, Mr Landon, it could kill him.'

It was meant as a joke, Arnold was certain, a black, humourless joke. But it left a nasty taste in Arnold's mouth. It also gave him another view of the heir to Willington Hall.

* * *

Now, the following morning, he thought back again over the final moments of the inquiry into the Penbrook Farm development. Certain things had been said, that bothered him.

Not by Sedleigh-Harmon, of course. He had risen to his feet to make some final comments regarding the environment. 'We have already made it clear that the ancient woodlands referred to by Miss Sauvage-Brown will not be affected. We have equally given assurances that, as can be seen from the plans, as little disruption as possible will be made, by the provision of access roads and service systems to the site when building commences beyond the ridge. The mediaeval nature of Penbrook Farm, well, there is little we can do about that and surely, Chairman, you will agree that progress must be made: we cannot continue to exist in a mediaeval society! And as for the pigsty slates commented upon so ably by the planning officer, and by which Miss Sauvage-Brown sets so much store, again I feel we can settle any problems there. If they are so important, my clients are prepared to preserve them in situ, properly fenced off, as a showplace. If this is not acceptable they are prepared to remove the whole sty, stone by stone, and re-erect it in a more suitable location. This way, the heritage will be preserved.'

'*Preserved*?' Mildred Sauvage-Brown's voice had risen to a hysterical yelp. 'You call that preservation? You and the rest of these bloody lunatics are throwing away the only things worth anything in modern society and you talk of preservation!'

Sarah Ellis had tapped at Mildred's arm, but the anger in her companion's veins would brook no control, and Sarah Ellis had subsided, clutching to her bosom her little dark book and rocking sadly in her seat.

'Don't let's have this mealy-mouthed crap about the preservation of the environment from land-hungry clods like Wilson and Livingstone, and their mouthpiece Sedleigh-Harmon,' Mildred had shouted, as the pandemonium around her grew. 'They're after making money. That's all. And they'll stoop to every low deal, every dirty trick to do that. The Minford Twilight Home! Who'll really benefit from that? Bloody Albert Minford! And who'll be doing the building over the ridge once you have desecrated Penbrook Farm? Tell me that! And how many other deals are cooking to keep councillors sweet? The Alnwick drainage scheme! The Amble marina! That bloody bridge at Wark! There are the pies, but whose are the fingers dabbling in them! And who's plucking out the cherries?'

It was at that stage the Chairman had hastily called the hearing to a close and Mildred Sauvage-Brown had made her determined lunge in Arnold's direction. It had been unexpected: he had hardly expected to be designated as a major enemy, but perhaps she felt he was in some curious way worse than the others, because he had declared sympathy with her stand. He had tried to get out of the doors in the rush, but she had managed to coil her thick stubby fingers in his shirt collar, ripping it, before he managed to make good his escape.

But it was not that which really bothered Arnold. He felt guilty, and a sense of shame touched him for his inability to help Mildred Sauvage-Brown and Sarah Ellis more positively; at the same time he wondered whether he had entirely done his duty. Had he devoted enough time to the ramifications of the case before it was presented to the hearing? Had he really carried out a sound enough check on the *background* to the Penbrook Farm application?

He fished out three files from the cabinet in the office of the Senior Planning Officer. The first was the file concerning the bridge at Wark: expensive, some claimed unnecessary, and certainly an eyesore when placed immediately alongside the thirteenth-century stone bridge it would render redundant. The building firm was Corey and Fairhurst; architects, Glinson's.

Nothing untoward there. He checked the tenders: they seemed in order. He turned to the second file.

Mildred Sauvage-Brown had shouted about the Alnwick drainage scheme. He looked at the file: he knew very little about it. The details were there: the castle stood on the hill above the town and the land to the north-east fell away into meadows through which the Aln ran to the sea at Alnmouth. That particular spot was visually romantic: one could see days of chivalry mirrored in the scene. But just north of the castle there were drainage problems in winter and the Aln regularly burst its banks in the spring floods. The work was to divert part of the watercourse, raise banks and construct new sewers. Builders: Wellington Bros; architects, Samuel and Hines. Tenders in order.

That left Amble. Arnold had already dealt with the file personally and he had detected nothing unusual in it. The application was young yet; newspaper notices had been placed, inviting tenders. There were three tenders already in, and he had not paid much attention to them since he would expect others to emerge. Now he looked at them more closely.

Corey and Fairhurst, the contractors for the Wark bridge.

That was all right: they were fairly big builders and well experienced in local authority contracts. The second bid was from a company he did not know. Floyd and Simson. He turned to the third tender. Again, a contracting firm with a pretty good record of local authority work — Nickerson's.

Arnold turned back to the second tender. Floyd and Simson. He stared at it, pondering. A limited company: managing director, E. Floyd; finance director, T. Simson. Something prickled at the back of his neck. A newspaper cutting, or a photograph, some time ago, a few years back . . . Floyd. There'd been a builder of that name in Newcastle, but the firm had merged . . . with whom?

Arnold closed the file, walked out into the corridor and obtained a cup of cool coffee from the vending machine. Its days were numbered, he thought darkly. Any time now, it would be brought to justice. He took the coffee back to his office.

From his window he had a narrow view of the gardens on the hill; above the gardens, wheeling against the morning sky, was a flock of fieldfares. Arnold watched them for a while, sipping his coffee, and his mind drifted back, sifting facts and memories . . . Floyd. A merger. It hadn't worked.

But that was all he could remember. Irritated, Arnold finished his coffee, replaced the files and then, hesitantly, made his way along the corridor and up the stairs to the Town Clerk's department. He still thought of it under that title although it had long since been changed to Department of Administration. He opened the door, walked in past the serried rows of law books and law reports and headed for the desk still occupied after thirty years by one Ned Keeton. The man's shaggy head came up as Arnold approached and the grey flyaway eyebrows twitched their surprise. 'Well, well, Arnold, don't see much of you up here!'

'Having once escaped, Ned, I'm always reluctant to return.'

'In case they catch you again, hey?' Ned Keeton grinned and shook his head. 'Me, I'll be escaping for good next summer. Time to go.'

'You're sixty-five?'

'Sixty. Early retirement. Had enough, stuck in here. Not like you, with the chance to get out and about. All I ever see outside this office is the magistrates' courtrooms. Hardly inspiring. But you didn't come up here to chat about my future. What can I do for you?'

Arnold hesitated. 'Councillors. There's a rule about declaring interests, isn't there?'

'So there is with officers, like you and me. Local Government Act 1972. Have to declare any interest they have in contracts entered into, or proposed, with the council.'

'What's meant by interest?' Arnold asked.

'Financial, of course. Directors. Shareholders. And it covers members of their families too, in some cases.' Slowly Arnold said, 'The declarations . . . they're contained in a register, of course.'

Ned Keeton scratched his head with his pen and gazed owlishly at Arnold. 'Oh yes, sniffing, are we? Fact is, in most cases the declaration is made in committee, so stated thereafter in the minutes, and provided the councillor hasn't voted on the issue that's the end of that. But a register . . . well, yes, there's a register. *Voluntary* register of interests. The canny ones who *think* they might be embarrassed in the future, they register their interests and that covers it. Of course,' he added slyly, 'people very rarely take a look at that register.'

'Do you think I could take a look?' Arnold asked.

'No reason why not,' Keeton replied with a wicked grin. 'Fully accredited, paid-up member, officer of the authority, all that kind of stuff. Access available. You want to tell me who you're looking for?'

'No.'

'Wise. Follow me.' Ned Keeton rose and shambled across the open-plan office, skirting the trailing plants that served as office dividers, until he reached the locked cabinet that stood outside the Chief Executive's office. 'Supposed to be highly confidential,' he said. 'But I got a key. Seniority, like. Help yourself, lad.'

Arnold helped himself.

There were only eight entries under the letter M. Albert Minford's entry dated back twelve years. Some of the interests noted had been excised as out of date, notably the interest he had held in his father's firm, since wound up. The more recent interests caught Arnold's attention.

Shareholder in Aln Enterprises, Ltd.

Director and shareholder in Ferrier, Glaze and Shannan, Ltd.

Shareholder in Corey and Fairhurst, Ltd.

Arnold closed the file and replaced it, locked the cabinet and went back to Ned Keeton. The grey-haired man cocked an inquisitive eyebrow. 'Find what you want?'

Arnold shrugged. 'Albert Minford is a shareholder in Corey and Fairhurst, the builders who tendered successfully for the Wark bridge.'

'He's declared the interest in the voluntary register?'

'He has.'

'Then that's it. All clean and above board. Can't be touched.'

'Did the planning committee know about his interest?' Arnold asked.

Keeton shook his head doubtfully. 'Doesn't matter whether they did or not. He wasn't on the planning committee. He declared his interest on the register. That's all he has to do other than not vote at council when the contract was ratified. Of course, it's a fact that people rarely *inspect* the register, and although the Chief Exec is supposed to bring the attention of the council to such matters it's a task that is observed in the breach rather than in the act, and the likelihood is that few people on council would even have *known* Minford had an interest in the Wark scheme. Which means . . .?'

'You tell me.'

'Well, I'm leaving this dung heap soon, and you can't quote me, and I'll even deny the conversation, but there's always the possibility, isn't there? I mean, a councillor putting a word in, doing some lobbying with the right people, maybe for a certain buried kickback that emerges later in an entirely different field — and with most of the members not knowing what's going on at all because the bloke pushing the scheme has no personal interest on the face of things and the guy who has an interest has declared it, isn't directly involved in the decision, and so his interest isn't even noticed. Even if he is active behind the scenes.'

'Minford?'

'I didn't say that, Arnold. I didn't say that.'

* * *

Arnold was left with a vague sense of unease. Mildred Sauvage-Brown had made wild claims at the hearing; he had undertaken a check but had come up with mere suppositions that Ned Keeton would not support in practical terms. It left Arnold in limbo: he felt he should act positively to support Sarah Ellis and Mildred Sauvage-Brown, for theirs were feelings close to his own, but it was his duty as a responsible planning officer to process the applications expeditiously.

Yet both considerations led to the same decision: an expression of sympathy, and the need for more concrete evidence of corruption, demanded that he visit Penbrook Farm once again, and encounter the formidable Miss Sauvage-Brown.

* * *

He set off after lunch to drive the twenty miles or so to Penbrook Farm. The afternoon skies were heavy, mackerel clouds deadening the horizon, and the lanes were quiet as he drove across country. His head began to ache and he was filled with a sense of gloomy foreboding: somehow, he felt he was getting involved in matters that lay beyond his control. The Senior Planning Officer was right about these things: a quiet life was all that was needed — no alarums, no excursions.

But ahead of him waited Mildred Sauvage-Brown, a woman to whom causes, preferably lost ones and little ones, were life blood.

He passed Ogle and took the road west, skirting the northern perimeter of Darras Hall until he neared Penbrook Farm. He could see the outline of the ancient wood on the hill and his heart was saddened. Whatever Sedleigh-Harmon might have claimed, that wood too would be at risk in time, as the old people's home and the residential sprawl beyond the ridge, became facts. He drove through the gateway, down towards the farmhouse, past the Shoulder of Mutton Mildred Sauvage-Brown had shown in her blackboard sketch, across the stream and Rivermead field, and he slowed as he reached the pigsty.

There were two cars parked near the farmhouse. Arnold stopped the engine, got out of the car and then he saw someone running up the lane towards the farmhouse.

She was wearing an elderly dress, the hem of which was torn and muddy. Her shoes were caked with mud also, and her grey hair straggled over her distraught features. To her narrow bosom she clutched the inevitable little book, and as he got out of the car she raised her hand to her face, brushing back the wild straggles to see him more clearly. There was a tear of relief in her voice when she called his name. He hurried forward, reaching out for her as she came to him, frail, weeping, terrified.

'Tell me,' Arnold demanded. 'What's happened?'

'Oh, I told her she shouldn't do it,' Sarah Ellis wailed, hollow-eyed. '*I told* her but she wouldn't listen, she's so much stronger than me.'

'What's happened?' Arnold asked again.

'She's down at the barn. You must help, Mr Landon, you *must* help!'

5

Arnold was nonplussed. He held Miss Ellis's shaking hands, trying to calm her down while he got some sense out of her. She was shaking violently, terrified and incoherent. She had dropped her little book and Arnold picked it up, stuffed it into his coat pocket, and tried to discover what had disturbed her.

'It's M-Mildred,' Sarah Ellis sobbed, leaning her head against Arnold's shoulder. 'She always overreacts so. I mean, I didn't know who he was, and there didn't seem to me to be any harm in it, but when Mildred came in she made me phone while she went down to the barn.'

'Is that where she is now?'

'Yes. But the way she's behaving . . . that poor man, it was awful, and Mildred was so rude, I just ran away again and cried, and then I saw you driving down the hill and I thought it was them and I came up to—'

'Them?'

'The press. The *Journal*.'

'Mildred asked you to phone the *Journal*?'

'She said this was the way to get things sorted out.' Inwardly Arnold groaned. He had the feeling that the events of the next few minutes could well mean publicity, newspaper coverage of the kind the Senior Planning Officer abhorred — and Arnold Landon, county planning officer of humble seniority, could well be right in the middle of it.

Instinct told Arnold he should stay well out of this situation; common humanity, on the other hand, dictated he should do something to assist the shaken Miss Ellis in her distress.

'The barn?' Arnold asked weakly.

'Oh, I'm *so* glad you'll help,' Sarah Ellis breathed. She grabbed his hand in a grasp surprisingly firm, and a moment later was trotting down the path with Arnold in tow like a reluctant lover. Sarah Ellis was a frail-looking old lady, but Arnold realized there were reserves of strength and steel in that elderly body.

They passed the first bend of the stream, crossed the narrow bridge below Barn Field, and above the hedge top Arnold could see the old timbers of the fifteenth-century barn, black and solid against the sky. From the spinney beyond, aware of the tension in the air, a great cloud of rooks swirled, clamouring their anger and distress, and darkening the sky like a smudge of smoke. The sound of their anxious cawing echoed from the craggy hill and found an answering chord in Arnold's chest. He could guess that trouble lay ahead.

They entered the gate and the path stretched ahead of them, muddied and difficult. Arnold dragged at Miss Ellis's hand. 'Do you think you need go any further?' he asked, aware that drama awaited at the barn.

'Please, Mr Landon, you *must* help!' she responded pinkly, panting in her anxiety. As though fearful he would desert her now, she gripped his hand even more tightly and Arnold was forced to squelch miserably behind her as she proceeded in her birdlike manner towards the dark barn looming ahead.

From this angle the barn had lost any charm it might have possessed for Arnold by virtue of its history. It seemed to lean against the hill, defying the ancient winds, and it was arrogant, fierce in its determination to survive.

As the path dipped in a fold in the field the barn rose higher in his vision to dominate the skyline and the arrogance became menace. Arnold could hear Sarah Ellis's breath tearing in her chest and her pace had slowed in spite of her quickening anxiety, but for himself there was a dull ache of presentiment.

The path curved, making its way with the contour of the slope towards the front entrance of the old barn. The door itself leaned crazily, broken on rusting hinges, and the timber of the construction gaped, wind-ravaged and weather-beaten.

Projecting through the doorway were the shafts of an old cart. The shafts were made of hickory, and the cart itself lacked one wheel. It leaned to one side drunkenly, and the wheel it still possessed lacked spokes. But Arnold's attention was swiftly drawn from the ancient cart. Standing at its rear was Mildred Sauvage-Brown.

She was at her most belligerent. She stood squarely, a righteous colossus, legs braced apart and ruddy countenance aflame with determination. She was carrying the shotgun with which she had first introduced herself to Arnold and his heart sank.

'What did you bring him here for?' Mildred Sauvage-Brown demanded indignantly of Sarah Ellis. 'I told you to phone the newspaper! Is there no sign of them yet?'

'Oh, Mildred—'

'Stop blabbing, Sarah! This is important! Media attention—'

Arnold stepped forward and the twin muzzles came up threateningly. 'Keep your distance, traitor!' she warned.

Arnold stared past her into the recesses of the barn. Just behind Miss Sauvage-Brown was a tripod, a theodolite lying on the ground. Beside the theodolite, his face contorted with terror and his hands locked together in supplication, was a man of small stature, on his knees, the eyes glaring wildly in his head. When he caught sight of Arnold he tried to speak but only a hissing sound came. 'Hell's flames,' Arnold said, shocked.

'I'll not warn you again, you traitor,' Mildred Sauvage-Brown snarled.

There was a gasping, choking sound from the man on his knees. He was wearing smart grey trousers tucked into green gumboots but they were stained with mud now and his hacking jacket was torn across the shoulder. His thin hair was plastered to his face in fear and his mouth was open, drooling terror. Arnold wet his lips. 'Who . . . who are you?'

The man tried to gasp a name but Mildred Sauvage-Brown spoke across the sound, contemptuously. 'His name's Carter. He's a surveyor. He's employed by those bloody rogues Wilson and Livingstone. You know what they had the gall to do? They sent him down here to Penbrook Farm with his damned instruments to make some preliminary calculations! If I'd been here at the time I'd have given him the boot! But Sarah—'

'Please, Mildred, this is all so unnecessary,' Sarah Ellis quavered, half-hiding behind Arnold.

'Now you leave this to me,' Mildred said. Her voice softened slightly, as she noted her companion's terror. 'You can go on back to the house if you like. 1 can handle all this.'

'What do you propose to do?' Arnold asked. 'Don't you think you can put that shotgun aside? Mr Carter is clearly . . . disturbed.'

'Damn right he's disturbed. But then, he came down here disturbing us, didn't he? Arrived when I was up on the hill, persuaded Sarah that he would do no harm, keep out of the way—'

'I was only . . . try . . . trying to do my job,' the little man broke in breathlessly.

'The hell with your job! Wheedled around Sarah, marched on down here with his bloody instruments and was all set up! I came down to the farmhouse, Sarah told me, and I realized the mileage we can get out of all this. Told her to phone the *Journal*, explain what I was going to do and then came down here to do it. What are *you* here for?'

Arnold thought the reasons for his presence irrelevant while Mildred Sauvage-Brown was still waving an armed shotgun in various directions. 'What are you going to do?'

'I'm going to make a statement to the press,' Mildred announced triumphantly. 'I'm going to get the kind of publicity we didn't get as a result of the hearing. Do you know there wasn't a single mention of that hearing in any of the local newspapers?'

'It's not normal for them to report—'

'Not a single bloody mention of our case! That'll be pressure, from Wilson and bloody Livingstone, I'm damned sure of it! All right, well, they've played their hand, and I'm going to play mine now.'

Arnold eyed the shotgun warily and the surveyor Carter whimpered as Arnold asked again, 'What do you intend to do?'

Mildred cleared her throat, hawked, spat, and ran the sleeve of her tweed jacket across her mouth, twitched the shotgun higher in the crook of her arm and grinned maliciously. 'I told you, I'm going to make a statement to the press. I'm going to state our case, then I'm going to keep this miserable little whippersnapper here in the barn, locked up, with this muzzle trained on him until either that bastard Wilson or his trained poodle Livingstone gets down here and apologizes for the act of trespass this miserable worm has committed in their name.'

'He . . . er . . . he came on with Miss Ellis's permission,' Arnold suggested.

'She was conned. She didn't know what she was doing.' The little man on his knees squirmed and appealed to Arnold, scrabbling in the dirty straw on the floor of the old barn. 'Hey, mister, get this crazy woman away from me, can't you? That gun—'

He subsided with a yelp as Mildred swung the shotgun in a dangerous arc, homing in on him. 'Shurrup, whippersnapper!' she commanded.

Arnold took a step forward, Sarah Ellis still clinging to his arm, weeping. 'Miss Sauvage-Brown, this is going too far.'

'The hell with that,' Mildred said confidently. 'We should have acted positively before now. Besides, it's too late for any arguing now. You hear?'

Arnold heard.

The rooks were creating bedlam in the spinney but on the distant wind he could hear the wail of a siren. It seemed that Sarah Ellis's phone call had had more than the desired effect. Perhaps alarmed by her tone, or concerned that this situation might develop into an even more newsworthy item if the police were involved, the *Journal* had clearly informed the local constabulary. They would be coming in force.

In a few minutes they came. Arnold groaned as the vehicles thundered down the lane and into Barn Field. There were four of them, two police cars and two others from which spilled three excited journalists and two photographers. The helmeted constables made a desultory attempt to keep them away from the approach to the barn but they eluded capture, running across the muddy field to get a better view — and better shots — of the dramatic scene unfolding at the entrance to the barn. One of the police officers was bareheaded, though in uniform. Clearly, he considered this was a method of defusing a dangerous situation. Equally clearly, he was in charge of the operation.

Mildred Sauvage-Brown cleared her throat and prepared for action. Arnold waited, helpless, aware that events had now gone far beyond his control, even if he had had any chance of controlling them earlier.

'Now then,' the bareheaded officer called as he strode purposefully towards the barn. 'What's going on?'

A photographer scrambled ahead of him, to one side, lugging his camera. He stopped to take a long shot of the scene and the officer scowled, waved an angry arm. 'Get the hell out of here!' He drew nearer to Arnold, scrutinized the sobbing Miss Ellis and asked, 'Who're you?'

Arnold completed the introductions, including the watchful Mildred Sauvage-Brown, and the bareheaded policeman nodded. 'I'm Chief Superintendent Fairbairn. I'm a blunt-speaking man. I don't like my afternoon off broken into like this and you better put that shotgun down, missus.'

The shotgun was waved negligently in his direction and the Chief Superintendent paled. 'Bloody hell,' he added.

'Don't want to talk to you, copper,' Mildred said coolly. 'But you better let those reporters come near and listen to me, and let them photographers get a few' shots or there'll be shots of a different kind flying around this barn.'

As the Chief Superintendent's neck purpled Arnold intervened hastily to explain the situation. The reporters gathered close, scribbling away as they listened. 'The easiest way, I think,' Arnold concluded,' 'is to let Miss Sauvage-Brown have her say, and then maybe the whole thing can be resolved peaceably.'

'I'll be wanting Wilson or Livingstone here,' Mildred warned, 'or this little feller back here stays with me!'

Chief Superintendent Fairbairn considered the matter. He raised a placatory hand. 'All right, we'll see what we can do, and if you want to make a statement to the lads here, well, you go ahead and do it, and then maybe we can talk a bit more, all right?'

Slightly mollified, but still suspicious, Mildred Sauvage-Brown nodded, and lifted the shotgun. The surveyor on his knees groaned faintly. 'This is what I want you all to print,' she said in a booming voice.

She proceeded to tell them. Arnold had heard it before, at the inquiry. She reeled off the story of the woodland, of the mediaeval farmlands comprised in Barn Field and Rivermead and the Shoulder of Mutton; she spoke of the slated pigsty and if Arnold winced when she denounced him as a traitor she clearly felt it was what he deserved. Arnold observed the reporters: they began eagerly, taking notes, but after a little while, as Mildred's rolling tones asserted the unique nature of Penbrook Farm and painted the property developers as villainous vandals the notes grew shorter, attention wandered to take in the scene behind Mildred's shotgun.

For the little surveyor, Carter, had decided to help himself.

Wrapped up in her demagoguery, Mildred had allowed herself to be distracted, half-turning away from Carter, declaiming to the reporters, and waving the gun towards the entrance to the barn. Carter had decided to take his chance. As she spoke he had got quietly up off his knees and was beginning to edge into the deeper recesses of the barn. For a moment Arnold thought the little man was making a bad mistake, but then he realized there must be some other means of egress from the barn, which had caught Carter's attention. The two uniformed constables stood quietly beside Chief Superintendent Fairbairn, Mildred continued her attack upon Wilson and Livingstone, Sarah sobbed, and Arnold held his breath.

'And now, all that remains,' Mildred boomed, ending her peroration, 'is for one of those two bastards to get here and apologize. Or else,' she added, raising her woollen-capped head, 'I'll keep this miserable little man in this barn until they do!'

There was a sudden clattering sound from the back of the barn. Mildred whirled around in consternation and for one long second was transfixed by the emptiness before her. The Chief Superintendent bellowed some incomprehensible order and the two constables stepped nervously forward just as Mildred, realizing what was about to happen, dashed into the darkness of the barn.

From the back of the barn Arnold heard one more terrified yell, a cracking, rending sound and then the sharp report of the gun as one of the twin barrels was discharged. He ran forward involuntarily, releasing Sarah's hand but the policemen rushed past him, shouldering him aside. Next moment he was half shoved forward by the pressing reporters, eager in spite of the gunshot to get closer to events, witness them first-hand. Within a trice they were retreating again as the policemen tumbled out.

Mildred Sauvage-Brown was almost beside herself with anger. Red in the face, woollen cap awry, she had reversed her grip on the shotgun and was now wielding it as a club, swinging it wildly in a wide arc, beating back the opposition, policemen and reporters, now that she had lost her prey. Fairbairn was shouting again, but there was a note of panic in his voice. Arnold realized that Mildred had probably not fired the shotgun deliberately; but more by accident as she stumbled in frustration into the darkness of the barn. Even so, she was in no mood to be reasoned with now, as she obviously felt herself in danger of physical assault and was determined to defend herself to the end.

One of the reporters cannoned into Arnold. A flashlight lit up the scene with a garish white light. The shotgun stock hissed wickedly through the air. Arnold felt the wind of it and stumbled back out of range, lurched against the door of the barn and the old wood, already splintered and gnawed at by wind and rain, gave way with a groaning, cracking sound, as though it were finally despairing of survival. Arnold lost his balance and went crashing backwards. As he fell there was a catching at his shoulder, he felt something tear, and realized his coat had been ripped by a protruding nail. He lay on his back, angry, thrusting an exploring finger in the long ragged slit in his coat.

His acquaintance with Mildred Sauvage-Brown was proving to be expensive: first, a perfectly sound shirt; now a perfectly good overcoat.

He was out of range for the moment. Beleaguered, Mildred Sauvage-Brown was retreating and as she backed off, step by step, whirling her shotgun like a club, she was tiring. Arnold was reminded of an elderly bovine, taunted by snapping dogs, but Mildred would have seen herself in quite a different light. The breath whistled in her sagging bosom, her square stance plodded her back in front of the pressing group of policemen, and she would see herself as a heroine, fighting for the preservation of all she believed in, against the advancing tide of vandals. But she was middle-aged: a condition that did not make up for commitment. She was short of breath: a condition that did not support her determination. The shotgun still swung, dangerously, but the timing was erratic, the length of arc less regular, and her wrists were dropping, the shotgun stock now swinging at the level of the policemen's waists. They clearly thought themselves particularly vulnerable at this stage, but Chief Superintendent Fairbairn had the confidence of command. Standing back, he shouted '*Now! Get her!*'

Seeking citations, two of his constables dived in.

The shotgun completed its arc. Mildred Sauvage-Brown was unable, tired as she was, to haul the swing and she staggered, off-balance. A flashgun bulb exploded again and a shoulder took her in the midriff. The breath came out of her in a great gushing sound and as the second brave policeman came tumbling in like an over-eager puppy, Mildred Sauvage-Brown collapsed on her back, mouth wide open in silent passion as two red-faced constables straddled her, attempting to hold her down and avoid her flailing arms.

Chief Superintendent Fairbairn was almost dancing in rage as he tried desperately to prevent the two photographers from recording the scene. Valiant protectors of the peace when faced with a menacing shotgun were one thing. The public was equally awed by headlines which read, above appropriate photographs: *Further examples of police violence* or *Three brave coppers subdue one old lady.*

The one old lady, on the ground, emitted great gouts of suppressed air. She stared wildly at the roof of the barn, but Arnold thought he detected an element of triumph in those eyes. He felt sorry for her, but then, he felt sorry for himself too.

He surveyed his own condition. Coat torn, trousers muddied and stained. Nothing good would come out of this business; nothing good for anyone.

Sarah Ellis was crying, hands clutched over her tear-stained face. The red-faced constables, breathing heavily, hoisted the gasping Miss Sauvage-Brown to her feet. She seemed suddenly exhausted and her shoulders were hunched, so they handled her more gently, aware that most of the fight had been knocked out of her.

Arnold was standing at the door of the barn as they led her out, one arm locked behind her back. She glared at Arnold, but he could not be sure she recognized him. She was already contemplating a courtroom, and another opportunity to state her case for Penbrook Farm.

'Oh, your poor coat,' Sarah Ellis said to Arnold, clutching to him suddenly like a survivor to a waterlogged plank.

Arnold inspected the tear gloomily. 'It'll be all right,' he said in an unconvinced tone. 'Don't worry about it.' He turned, disengaging himself gently, having had enough of the Sarah Ellises and the Mildred Sauvage-Browns for the moment. 'You'd better go back with the constable.'

The policeman was large, sympathetic, and eager to make amends for assaulting her companion. 'Come on, lady, I'll take you back to the farm and you can tell me all about it.'

'What'll happen to Mildred?' she trembled.

The constable hesitated. He glanced at the forbidding back of his superior officer, but Chief Superintendent Fairbairn was still clucking at the photographers, warning them he'd be speaking to their editor. 'I shouldn't worry too much,' the constable offered. 'There'll be some accounting to do but, well, she didn't actually *shoot* anyone, did she? Look.'

Arnold and Sarah Ellis followed the direction of his pointed finger. The surveyor, Mr Carter, was a distant figure. He had decided not to wait around to press charges. Having shouldered his panic-stricken way out of the back of the barn, bursting through the rotten wood, he was now to be seen legging it across Barn Field, heading at pace for the lane and his car.

Arnold could hardly blame him.

The constable took Sarah Ellis's arm and marched along with her through the mud of the field, while the small platoon ahead escorted Mildred Sauvage-Brown towards the police car. Arnold trudged along behind Sarah Ellis, gloomy and despondent at the turn of events. The Senior Planning Officer was bound to hear all about the fracas.

He shoved his hands in his pockets and became aware he still had something belonging to Miss Ellis. As they walked up the lane Arnold caught up with her, drew the little book from his pocket and looked at it. The book had a reddish-brown cover and seemed quite old. Some of the pages seemed to be loose.

'Miss Ellis, don't forget this.'

She clutched at it gratefully, managed a smile of thanks and the constable led her in through the gate of the farm-house. Arnold walked towards his car, peeling off his damaged overcoat. He unlocked the car and threw the coat on to the back seat.

The first of the police cars was driving up the lane towards him, heading for the main road above. Mildred SauvageBrown was in the back seat, incarcerated between the two burly constables. There couldn't be much room on that seat, Arnold thought to himself. He stepped back as the car drew near.

Mildred Sauvage-Brown had recovered her wind and her enthusiasm. Undeterred by her arrest, she leaned forward, recognizing Arnold as the car drove past. 'We shall overcome!' she shouted at him. 'I'm not finished yet!'

Arnold did not doubt it.

'We shall overcome!' she repeated in a high voice. 'Those bastards will get Penbrook Farm only over my dead body!'

The police car picked up speed to master the rising ground in the lane. Mildred Sauvage-Brown was still shouting. Her words drifted back to Arnold, above the distance cawing of the disturbed rooks in the spinney beyond Barn Field.

'Only over my dead body . . .'

CHAPTER THREE

1

The *Scarborough Advertiser* was not so insular that it did not carry national news; northern news tended to reach the front page, and so Arnold was not surprised when he received an irate telephone call from the Senior Planning Officer.

'I mean, what on earth is going on? What were you doing there at all — and getting *involved* in the situation!'

'It really was accidental,' Arnold replied weakly. 'I was just—'

Just nothing! I have to make it clear, Arnold: we in the department must not get into controversial situations. We must be seen to be independent, professional, damn it! Let the politicians and their ilk rant and rave, we must maintain a discreet silence, maintain a dignified professionalism, give discreet advice — and have nothing to do with the Mildred Sauvage-Browns of this world!'

With the last sentiment, Arnold was in hearty agreement. The woman aroused feelings of annoyance and resentment in him. Her aggressiveness, confidence and self-righteousness caused prickles of anger at the back of his neck, and her loud-mouthed claims of corruption in local government were of the kind that irritated him because they were so difficult to substantiate or dispute. He felt exposed. If there were any shady dealings on the part of people like Minford, Arnold felt he had to make them public as part of his moral duty, but he had no doubt that the Senior Planning Officer was not of the same mind. 'Circumspection,' the Senior Planning Officer warned. 'Circumspection.' It was another word for discretion, and shorthand for minding one's own business.

Mildred Sauvage-Brown possessed neither discretion, nor circumspection — and she intended minding everyone's business. Arnold groaned when he saw the news in the local newspaper the following evening. There had been a scene in the magistrates' court. Miss Sauvage-Brown had been hauled up before the local bench on a charge of disturbing the peace. Clearly, the police were hesitant about bringing a firearms charge against her, and the unfortunate surveyor, mindful of his own manly reputation, had obviously declined to press charges of assault and battery. It would have required only an assurance from the lady in question that she would refrain from further disturbances and she would have been bound over to keep the peace — which meant she would go free.

That was not Miss Sauvage-Brown's style. She had taken the opportunity to launch yet another attack on Wilson, Livingstone and Councillor Minford. She had repeated her vague statements about local government corruption. When the chairman of the bench had remonstrated, she had reminded him of his own involvement in the education committee scandal of two years previously and had called into question his moral obligations, one of which she suggested, should be resignation from his position as Justice of the Peace as being no fit and proper person to hold such a situation.

It was not a suggestion calculated to please the magistrate. He committed her to the cells for a month. After a hurried and nervous approach from the Clerk to the Court, the red-faced magistrate changed his verdict and bound her over for psychiatric reports. When she responded by telling him with some force what he could do with psychiatric reports, his face got redder and he committed her to prison for contempt of court in spite of the chalkiness of the Clerk of the Court's features.

Bail was eventually fixed at three hundred pounds. All in all, Arnold concluded, the proceedings seemed to have been confused and exciting. Any sensible woman would have backed down, taken the easy way out of court. Mildred Sauvage-Brown had not, and had made the kind of headlines she desired.

In the afternoon session, it seemed, the chairman of the bench had retired from the courtroom, saying he felt ill. There was a hint in the newspaper account that his legs were unsteady. Arnold did not blame him. In such trying circumstances, he too would have been tempted to take a few stiff whiskies at lunchtime.

She was still on his mind when he did the Saturday morning shopping in Morpeth. It caused him to forget several items and he was in a niggly frame of mind when he was forced to return twice to the little corner shop he frequented, for coffee, and later, some potatoes.

Accordingly, his normal equanimity was in short supply when he felt the hand buffeting his shoulder and he heard the booming voice behind him. *'Weel, are ye gangin' doon the yelhoose ter wet yer neb wi' yer marrer?'*

Arnold turned, coldly, but with fire in his veins. 'What I really can't stand,' he said, 'is people who are particularly careful about their accent and who would be annoyed if someone tried to imitate their rounded vowels, and yet who feel it's clever to try to use Geordie vernacular, and fail miserably at it!'

'Hey, hey, man,' Freddie Keeler stepped back, raising both hands in mock dismay. 'All I was doing was being a bit friendly, like. It's been a hard morning, plenty inquiries, no house sales, and I'm on my way for a pint. You want me to rephrase it? I'll do it, Arnold, just for you.' He struck a pose, left foot forward, left hand extended, head cocked on one side. 'Well, are you going down to the pub to have a drink with your friend?'

Arnold smiled, in spite of the simmering annoyance in his veins. He knew the sharpness of his response had not really been the result of Freddie Keeler's request: there were other reasons, connected with Miss Sauvage-Brown's incarceration and yet generally undefined. 'I'm sorry, Freddie. You sort of caught me on the hop, then. You're going to The Black Bull?'

The tubby estate agent nodded. 'No better place.'

'I'll join you. Just let me lock up the car.'

It was only just after midday and the lounge bar was filling rapidly with Saturday lunchtime drinkers. As Keeler bought the drinks Arnold found some seats in the corner of the warm room, away from the droning of the horse race commentator on the television set suspended above the bar. Keeler stood there for a short while, watching the progress of the race; at its conclusion he came across to Arnold with an expression of disgust on his face. 'Typical,' he muttered. 'Never take a hot tip from a client. He knows you're trying to screw him on price, so he sets you up in revenge by giving you an also-ran as a dead cert.'

'Didn't know you were interested in horses.'

'Anything that'll make me money. Didn't you know that about estate agents? Anyway, you still got the glum face. Here's your beer. Drink up and smile.'

Arnold sipped at his beer. 'I'm sorry about that flare-up outside. I—'

'Say no more, dear boy. I can guess what brought it on. I saw the papers. I guess your boss ain't gonna be too pleased, as they say.'

Arnold grimaced. 'That's one way of putting it. And at the moment things don't seem to be dying down.'

Freddie Keeler caressed his nose, as though reminding himself of the red, broken veins that had started to accumulate under the skin. 'Mildred Sauvage-Brown. She seems quite a character.'

'She is.'

'And noisy.'

'How do you mean?'

Freddie Keeler grinned. 'Well, she certainly got the magistrate's goat, didn't she? Probably striking too close to home. You reckon he got stoned at lunchtime to recover?'

Arnold smiled. 'Seems like it. But you think she *was* getting near the truth?'

Keeler shrugged. 'There was a fuss a while back about him and some dinner lady at one of the schools . . . But she's just as noisy in your field, from all I can gather.' Arnold hesitated. He had a feeling the Senior Planning Officer would not approve, but slowly, he asked, 'Do you think she's right about the other . . . allegations?'

Freddie Keeler sipped at his gin and tonic and then looked at Arnold carefully. He always gave an impression of being a cheerful, fun-loving man, a good drinking companion, one who viewed life as something to be enjoyed and not taken too seriously. But he was a good businessman, and Arnold had occasionally wondered whether Freddie Keeler was a deal more sagacious than he appeared. The bonhomie could be a front, a cover for shrewdness. 'Allegations . . . Smoke and fire, isn't it, Arnold?'

'I could also come back at you about old wives' tales.'

Keeler's eyes held hints of calculations. He rubbed at his balding pate. 'I don't know too much about what's been said by the good lady, but I do hear it involves a couple of businessmen.'

'Wilson and Livingstone,' Arnold supplied. 'Do you know them?'

'By reputation. Not exactly done much business with them but I've seen them work, and one of them at fairly close hand.'

'How do you mean?'

Keeler hesitated, uncertain suddenly whether to go on. Then he shrugged. 'Well, I'll tell you. I've always felt you're a bit . . . naive about some things, so maybe it's time your eyes were opened to the wicked ways of the world. You ever heard of the Auction Act of 1969?'

'I'm not sure,' Arnold said cautiously.

'Its full title is the Auctions (Bidding Agreements) Act,' Keeler said, and added feelingly, 'I can quote it almost *verbatim*.'

'What's it say?'

'The act says that if a dealer gives anyone a 'consideration' — you know what consideration means?'

'Sort of payment.'

'Right. If a dealer gives anyone a consideration for abstaining from bidding at an auction sale a criminal offence is committed on the part of the dealer and the person receiving the consideration.'

'So?'

Keeler stroked his nose thoughtfully. 'Well, the act has never been particularly popular with auctioneers and estate agents and dealers. You see, in the old days knock-out agreements weren't illegal.'

'Knock-out agreements?'

'An agreement between intending bidders not to bid against each other. The idea was,' Keeler explained, 'that a group of people got together at an auction, only one of them made a bid, the item got knocked down to him at a fairly low price and then the group could have a *private* auction among themselves later, when a higher price was likely to be gained. The difference in the price could be split between the bidders.'

'And the seller in the first place was cheated out of the proper sale price?'

Keeler shuffled uncomfortably. 'Well, he had his own remedy — he could always fix a reserve price on the article. Anyway, be that as it may, fact is the old legal position was changed, it's illegal to have such rings these days, but . . .'

'It still goes on?' Arnold asked after a short pause.

Keeler sipped at his gin. 'You can say that again. You see, up around here, where you got so many big houses, with old ladies dying off all the time, there's a treasure house of antiques. Not too many people know their true value, and some of the London dealers are unscrupulous bastards. So there's more than a few people up here who've banded together to keep things quiet, keep the London mob away, and do our own private deals.'

'*Our?*'

Keeler waved his glass negligently. 'I been involved a few times.'

Arnold paused. 'What's this got to do with Mildred Sauvage-Brown's allegations?'

'Not a lot. But we were talking about Wilson and Livingstone.'

'They're involved?'

Freddie Keeler shook his head. 'Not centrally. They're just amateurs, if you like: fringe people. But they're on the circuit list, and they get invitations to the bidding rings.'

'Why?'

There was a roar from the end of the bar as another horse race ended. Keeler glanced back dolefully and shook his head. 'Suckers . . . Why do they get invited, you ask? I asked myself, some time back. And I got a theory. You see, I knew Livingstone way back. He's done well.'

'In what way?'

'He's a Byker lad, you know, though you wouldn't guess it now. He was a tearaway as a kid, quick to give you a *nasty dunch on the jaa*, and he talked like that, I'm telling you! Bright lad, though, and he left Tyneside for a few years, came back and moved upwards, rapidly.'

Arnold thought back to his first meeting with the tall, reddish-haired Livingstone. He remembered the athletic force of the man and could believe he could have been active in the Byker terraces. There was certainly no trace of a Geordie accent now, however: the man was controlled, and tough. 'His climb . . . was that in the property business?'

'That's right. I think he must have got going as a jobber builder down south, made a few thousand quid, expanded, then came back north and joined Wilson. That's when he really began to do well.'

Wilson, the frosty-eyed, middle-aged businessman and his younger, more muscular lieutenant. 'So what's the involvement with the auction rings?' Arnold asked.

'I told you. Just amateurs, really. And a couple of times I've had the feeling maybe they're conning us, using us to set up their own deals. Anyway, fact is, my personal contacts with them have been at the rings. Not that I attend many of them, of course, but either Wilson, or Livingstone, or on occasions both of them, tend to be there. Not spending much, generally, but once in a while . . .'

'A hobby for them?'

'For Wilson, I would guess. Livingstone . . . I'm not so sure. I think he takes it seriously. But I get the impression that character takes everything seriously. He's the kind who's got to win, you know? And maybe, if you take his Byker background into account, he'll do just about anything to do it.' He considered the matter for a moment, staring thoughtfully into the puddle of gin and tonic in his glass. 'Yes . . . old Wilson, he's a canny old buzzard and not above a bit of skulduggery, but it would be done at a distance, and smoothly, a knife between the shoulder-blades. Livingstone's a different kettle of fish. He'd do things *personally*, and he'd do it with a bludgeon. He'd like the sound of crunching bone . . . Mine's a gin and tonic again, Arnold.'

Arnold made his way to the bar. While he waited to catch the attention of the barman he was vaguely aware of the television discussion on the merits of various football teams. The Senior Planning Officer was a supporter of Newcastle United. It puzzled Arnold: association football was a mystery to him, as were most sporting activities. He assumed it was due to something missing in his genes.

He gave Freddie Keeler his gin and tonic, placed his own half pint on the table and sat down. 'You read the newspaper accounts about the outburst from Miss Sauvage-Brown?'

Keeler nodded. 'The reports weren't very specific. Just making sure there was no libel suit, I reckon. It was easy to pick out Wilson and Livingstone, of course, but it looked to me like the local government corruption stuff had been edited out. Even so, I suppose it's Councillor Minford she's screaming about.'

'That's right. Have you had many dealings with him?'

Keeler shook his head. 'Not a lot. I mean, he's been in the building business way back, and I did a fair amount of work with his old man, but Minford closed down the business and went into politics. Had a fair bit of cash salted away: what his father had made, and he married someone who had her own cash.'

'Wasn't she involved in the building business as well?'

'Oh yes, I mean that's how they got together, the story goes. She was the daughter of that character who built up that Gateshead firm . . . what the hell was his name?'

'I can't say.'

'No matter. The company was a flourishing one — Jarrow Development Corporation — and they made a bomb in the sixties. He was a contemporary of old Minford and the two got together, decided upon a merger and it was about that time that Albert Minford got shacked up with his present wife. Eileen . . . damn it, what was her name? She'd been married before. She's more than a few years older than Minford so the story was he was as much interested in her cash as in her body — and she had a grown-up son. Her husband died a long time back, and she'd been working with her father . . .'

'I seem to recall something about it at the time,' Arnold admitted. 'Weren't they on the fringe of the Poulson scandals in some way?'

'Never brought to book, but there were a lot of fringe activities in *that* area,' Keeler said with emphasis. 'Thank God I was never involved. Anyway, like I was saying, Jarrow Development and Minford's firm went into a merger arrangement, but something went sour and by the time the two old men had died the new company was falling apart. They cut their losses, went into liquidation, and the principals got out with enough cash to live on and more. Minford married his

Eileen, with her grown-up son, walked into a political life, and she . . . damn it, that's right, she started another firm in her own right. Went into business with her son.'

Arnold frowned. Something stirred muddily at the back of his mind. He thought back, aware there was something he should remember but it escaped him. Annoyed, he put it aside.

'You've heard no rumours that would back up Miss Sauvage-Brown's allegations?'

'Don't really know what the allegations are,' Keeler confessed. 'But my guess would be she doesn't really know herself. I've had dealings from time to time with these conservationists. They see fascist pigs in every farmyard. They go for the jugular without much compunction and it's nothing to do with finesse. A slashing stroke, believe me, and the blood spurts everywhere. Difficult stains to remove. They know it. And they don't care. Bloody eccentrics. They'll do anything to save their bloody woodlands, hayricks and hen-houses. Come across any old barns lately?'

Recognizing the mischief in the estate agent's tone, Arnold refused to rise to the bait.

* * *

Arnold was not sure what he had got out of his conversation with Freddie Keeler. He had been vaguely aware of the existence of auction rings: from time to time there had been reports of prosecutions, but everyone agreed that such arrangements were extremely difficult to prove. The only chance the police had was to find someone prepared to inform on the others; alternatively, there was the chancy business of following dealers when they left auctions and checking to discover whether they were meeting in secret as a group for the 'knock-out'. The trouble there was that if the meeting took place on private premises the police had no right of entry.

But even if Wilson and Livingstone were involved in such activity it could essentially have no bearing on the future of

Penbrook Farm. Mildred Sauvage-Brown was making vague accusations but so far there was no factual basis for them to Arnold's knowledge. The Senior Planning Officer would advise him he was wasting his time. Freddie Keeler had characterized the lady's behaviour as eccentric, and perhaps deliberately vague because there was no basis for her claims.

As for Arnold himself, he was questioning his own motivation. He was sympathetic towards Sarah Ellis and the case made out by Mildred Sauvage-Brown for Penbrook Farm. But was that sympathy now causing him to go too far with his suspicions? Was he subconsciously taking the side of the two ladies, unjustly, when the two businessmen and the councillor in the case were doing nothing wrong?

He could not be certain and his own doubts made him depressed and unhappy. He drove home from his meeting with Freddie Keeler in a doubtful frame of mind. The skies had darkened, there was rain in the wind, and he suspected he would be able to do no work in the garden, as he had planned, that afternoon.

He made some lunch for himself and sat down in the small sitting-room of his bungalow. There was an old film on television: he watched it for a while and then drifted off into an uneasy sleep.

He woke with a start at four o'clock. The room was dim, and the black and white images of the film sent dancing shadows across the walls.

The files. He remembered looking at them; one in particular. A building firm, Floyd and Simson.

Freddie Keeler had been unable to remember the name of the man who had built up the Jarrow Development Corporation. But Arnold remembered now: Kenneth Floyd.

And his daughter had married a man called Simson.

A slow surge of anger crawled through Arnold's veins.

He walked out into the hallway and put on his coat. He got the car out and drove down to Morpeth. He walked into the police station and got out his cheque-book.

Then he posted bail for Mildred Sauvage-Brown.

2

The trouble with Sunday newspapers was that they had time to devote to digging up further facts, embellishing them, and producing 'reasoned' articles, complete with the background to events. Arnold was horrified on the Sunday morning to find that his picture was in the paper.

It was not a good one, and a couple of years out of date.

It had been taken, and used, at the time of the debate on the Old Barn at Rampton, when he had achieved a brief television fame. The photograph had not pleased him and it had rendered the Senior Planning Officer apoplectic. It was now reprinted, together with a rehashed account of the events at Penbrook Farm.

There was also a photograph of Penbrook Farm, taken from the old wildwood and showing the spread of the mediaeval fields that Mildred Sauvage-Brown was attempting to save.

She appeared centrally, dominating the article itself.

Arnold guessed the shot must have been taken at Penbrook Farm by one of the photographers present at the time: the man clearly had taken advantage of his presence to do some entrepreneurial shooting he had not submitted to his own newspaper.

It did not show Mildred Sauvage-Brown in a good light. Her mouth was open, roaring; a burly constable held her left arm, and she appeared to be swinging a right hook in the direction of Chief Superintendent Fairbairn. His features expressed alarm, but that could have been due to the poor focusing of the picture: in the excitement of the moment the photographer had probably got his focal lengths wrong.

There was also a print of Sarah Ellis. She appeared to be crying. She was standing in the front doorway of the farmhouse, raising one arm in protest to cover her features, unsuccessfully, and clutching in the other hand the inevitable book, as though it would save her.

Disturbed, Arnold took the phone off the hook in case the Senior Planning Officer was so moved as to ring him in high dudgeon, got himself his copy of *Archaeologia Cantiana*, removed to the small bedroom he had furnished as a study and failed to concentrate for the next two hours.

* * *

The Senior Planning Officer finally contacted him at ten on Monday morning.

He was fairly polite, for the Senior Planning Officer. He was certainly succinct. And direct. In fact, Arnold could not remember when the Senior Planning Officer had made himself clearer. If there was any more trouble, any more publicity, any more *unseemly* involvement in matters scandalous, Arnold could expect a redeployment within the local authority.

And *then* there'd be no more gallivanting around the hills of Northumberland, to *everyone's* relief.

Nor did his philanthropic gesture — if that was how he could describe it to himself — regarding Mildred Sauvage-Brown, give him any satisfaction. At lunchtime a rather large and curious police sergeant visited his office at Morpeth. He eyed Arnold with some suspicion.

'Mr Landon?'

'That's right.'

'I'm Sergeant Entwistle. You . . . er . . . you posted bail on Saturday for a Miss Sauvage-Brown.'

Arnold hesitated. 'I did.'

'She wasn't too pleased.' The sergeant eyed Arnold again, curiously. 'She gave us quite a time when we told her she could leave. Said she had no intention of . . . how did she put it? Relinquishing her martyrdom. Yeh, that was it.'

'It sounds like her.'

'I brought your cheque around, sir. We . . . that is, the Super thought you ought to have it back . . . with a word of warning.'

'About what?'

'About getting mixed up with funny people like Miss Sauvage-Brown.'

'She's not funny.'

'I think the Super meant . . . eccentric, sir.'

Arnold took the proffered cheque. 'I'm surprised you brought it round to me.'

'Not usual, but like the Super said, a word of warning.

'Is the lady still in the cells?' Arnold asked.

The police sergeant shook his head; 'Naw. I think it was one thing to take a stand. Maybe she'd been reconsidering her position Saturday, except that the news that bail had been posted meant she got the idea someone was trying to interfere, take away her rights, sort of. But having taken the decision to stay . . . well, Saturday night ain't the same as Friday night, sir.'

'How do you mean?'

'Clientele gets a bit rougher. A few of the football crowd, one or two drunk and disorderly; noisy it gets, and smelly too. I think she kind of changed her mind about ten on Saturday night.'

'You mean she left?'

'Decided to pay her own recognizances. Paid up, cleared off, gone home, I shouldn't be surprised. But a gentleman like you, sir, you shouldn't get mixed up in things like this . . . people like her. So the Super reckons.'

It was a sentiment the Senior Planning Officer would have heartily endorsed.

The visit was not the last of the surprises Arnold faced that day, however. At four in the afternoon he received another visitor, just as he was despondently clearing his desk prior to going home. It was Henry Willington.

It was clear from the moment that the man walked into his office something was wrong. His wind-tanned skin seemed to have paled, and held a greenish look. Arnold remembered the lines on his face but they appeared to have deepened, cicatrices of doubt around his eyes and mouth. His pale brown eyes reflected that doubt: they seemed to be seeking something long since lost, the certainty of youth. At Arnold's invitation he sat down. His left hand was shaking slightly.

'Are you all right?'

'I think so.'

Arnold watched the man for a few minutes and then walked across to the filing cabinet. The Senior Planning Officer would not have approved, but Arnold kept a bottle of whisky among the files, for emergency purposes. There had only been a couple of occasions when he had felt the need to use the bottle: this was clearly one of them. He did not ask Willington: rather, he merely poured him a drink in the tumbler he kept in his desk and then sat down. 'You'd better tell me.'

'I've just been along the corridor.'

Arnold knew, suddenly, without being told. 'It can't have been a surprise, surely.'

'No, but when it happens . . .' The pale brown eyes tried to focus on Arnold but failed. Willington lifted the glass, sipped vaguely at the whisky, hardly aware of what he was doing. 'When it happens, it's unexpected, really, and the forms . . .' He sipped the whisky again. 'Seeing the forms, it sort of brings it home to you.'

'When did it happen?'

'Yesterday. He was going through his usual routine. Did the same thing every Sunday morning. He used to get up about seven, have some toast and coffee, fuss about in his study for a while and then sit down to read the papers. He called to me . . .'

His glance became dulled, introspective, and Arnold felt a vast sympathy for the man. He had been bitter about Patrick Willington, angry that his father had depleted the estate, wanted to get his hands on it to put things right, but now, when the opportunity was coming his way it had the taste of ashes. 'He was able to speak?' Arnold asked, to break the silence.

Henry Willington nodded. 'Oh yes, he was quite lucid for a while. But I . . . I knew there was something wrong. And then he choked, dropped the papers, and I ran to get some water . . . When I came back, he was dead.'

'Heart attack?'

The pale brown eyes were vague again. 'I called the doctor immediately. He was there before lunchtime. He said there'd probably have to be a post-mortem . . . Mr Landon, he looked so different!'

'It wasn't necessary for you to come in today,' Arnold said gently. 'It could have waited . . .'

'No.' Henry Willington shook his head with a sudden vehemence. 'The things he said . . . I had to find out.' He paused again, distressed, and yet giving Arnold the impression he was almost standing outside himself, watching a shadow play — Patrick Willington, Henry Willington, Arnold Landon. 'I went through the papers in his study.'

Arnold hesitated. It was none of his business, but it was clear that Henry Willington wished to talk. 'Did you find that . . . his affairs were as bad as you feared?'

'I already knew they were bad. I merely found the confirmation.' He sighed, almost in despair. 'I knew his father before him had left the estate in a mess, but I think it could have been turned around, the whole situation, if only my father had possessed an ounce of business sense. Or even when I came back, an ounce of . . . he would never listen you see.'

'The estate can't be saved?'

Henry Willington shrugged. 'There are still some properties to be sold, but it will be a long haul. I came in today to talk to the Registrar of Deaths, and to have a word with you about the planning application for the sawmill.'

'It can easily be withdrawn now,' Arnold said.

'That's good. It would never have worked, would it? He was so . . . *incompetent*.' The word had a sudden urgency that took Arnold by surprise. He had felt that Henry Willington's emotions were of sadness, loss and anxiety about the future. But now he knew there were still elements of the resentment he had detected that day at Willington Hall, when Henry had talked so bitterly of his father.

Henry Willington finished his whisky and set the glass down on the desk, regaining control of himself. 'You'll arrange for withdrawal of the application, then?'

'It's no problem. And if we can help in any way over the estate itself . . . as far as planning is concerned . . .' Arnold stumbled over the words, at a loss, but Henry Willington hardly seemed to hear him.

'There's no money of any consequence,' he said slowly. 'About thirty thousand in the bank. That'll not even cover the Hall's running expenses. What it requires is an injection of capital, wise investment . . .'

'Perhaps the sales you engender—'

'No.' The tone was positive, the eyes clearing, a little panicked wildness entering his glance as though the very thought of relinquishing Willington Hall terrified him. 'No. That won't be necessary. I'll find a way. There must be . . . there will be a way. The family have always rallied around in the past, in the old days, but Patrick was so stupid, so criminally stupid that he lost the chance, the only real chance there was at the time . . . And now . . .' Willington stared at Arnold with a sudden clarity, as though he were seeing him for the first time. Yet Arnold was left with the feeling that it was not Arnold that Henry Willington saw.

* * *

After the man had gone, instead of rushing home Arnold poured himself a drink and sat on in the darkened office. The rest of the staff had left, but he had a key, and he was disinclined to leave.

He sipped his whisky and thought of Henry Willington and Patrick Willington and a man who had died years ago in the Yorkshire Dales. A man and his son . . . a difficult relationship. That between Patrick and Henry had certainly been soured, by the older man's fanciful dreams and incompetent bungling, and by the son's resentments, the knowledge that he could do better if only he were given the opportunity. Now that the chance had come it was probably too late; the old man was gone; leaving an unwelcome legacy.

It had been so different for Arnold. He would never lose the legacy his father had left him: of warmth, of caring; of the love for things that were disappearing, of traces of ancestors who had long since passed away. There had been no resentments, just a deep sense of loss when Arnold's father had died; yet even that loss was never to be deep, because his father had left so much of himself in Arnold.

The thought caused tears to prickle at the back of Arnold's eyes: the knowledge that he would never, really, be alone.

Arnold should have gone home at that point, but instead he reached for the bottle and poured himself another drink, unwilling to lose the moment and the memory. His mind drifted back over the days he had spent in the dales with his father, tramping through the disused farms and the dying villages. He was a child again, with a child's emotions, as he felt the whisper of a breeze on his cheek and saw the morning sun gild the hills.

He had had a sandwich at lunchtime and nothing since, but the whisky was warming him, and he felt no hunger. A shaft of moonlight crept through the window and outside, he knew, there would be a hint of frost in the air.

At nine o'clock, the bottle empty, he rose unsteadily from his chair.

He had difficulty finding his keys to lock the door behind him. He had greater difficulty finding his car keys. Once inside the car, however, his confidence grew and with it came a strange sense of resentment.

He did not like Mildred Sauvage-Brown. She was the worst kind of conservationist: the noisy kind. She brayed her beliefs from the rooftops and antagonized people. She gloried in her eccentricity, claimed it as commitment, and gave a cause a bad name.

Moreover, she was arrogant. She was the kind of woman who would never take advice, who would always be certain she was right, who would override poor little mice like Sarah Ellis, and who would mercilessly use people like Arnold Landon to further her own ideas.

She was also insensitive, he concluded, refusing to accept a helping hand, too proud to allow Arnold Landon to salve his own conscience by posting her bail.

She needed to be told so — to her face.

Sober, Arnold knew, he would never be able to do it.

Drunk, as he was, it was a different matter. Drunk, he could debate with philosophers, insult kings. And certainly put bloody Mildred Sauvage-Brown down a peg or two.

He started the car, drove away from headquarters and dared a police car to stop him as he swung out of the town, up the hill and across to the quiet country lanes that led towards Penbrook Farm.

The hedgerows seemed to lead him on whitely, and there was a gay sparkle of frost in the road. He passed one or two cars, and they dazzled him with their headlights, but the exhilaration in his blood gave him the confidence to continue, warmed him with the satisfaction of knowing that he would be able to tell Mildred Sauvage-Brown what a fool she had made of herself at the hearing and afterwards, and particularly at the farm when she had so frightened the little surveyor Carter. He would be able to say, loftily, that he had been moved by the highest motives in dealing with the matter of her bail, and she had showed crass and insensitive stubbornness in refusing the gesture. And then he would sweep out, back to the car, leaving her speechless.

The thought gave him a warm glow.

The gate to Penbrook Farm was open and Arnold negotiated the track with confidence. The stream glittered in the moonlight as he swung down past Rivermead field and the farmhouse was a dark, humped shape at the bottom of the lane. He parked the car, killed the engine, switched off the lights and got out of the driving seat.

There were no lights at the farm.

Arnold hesitated. No lights, no people, he reasoned, and the glow inside him began to fade. He stood beside his car, uncertain. The battered car was parked outside the house, and the Land Rover was also in the lane. It was possible the two women had gone to bed, but on the other hand there could be a room at the back of the farmhouse, where he would see no light from the lane. He closed the car door and walked towards the entrance.

The gate was open. Again Arnold paused. The warmth he had experienced during the drive was evaporating at the same rate as his confidence. He was not certain, now, that he desired a confrontation with Mildred Sauvage-Brown: at the same time, he would feel extremely foolish and cowardly if he turned back, having come so far. He marched forward with a sudden resolution and knocked on the door.

There was a hollowness about the sound that surprised him. He waited, but there was no reply. He tried again, knocking harder and then, without quite knowing why, he turned the old-fashioned handle of the door and he realized it was off the latch.

The door swung slowly open and Arnold stood framed in the entrance to the dark passageway beyond. There were no lights visible and although the moonlight penetrated the windows of the room on the left it gave little illumination to the stone-flagged passageway itself.

Arnold could not recall seeing the light switches when he had visited the farmhouse previously. He hesitated, not knowing what to do.

'Hallo?'

His voice echoed, fluttering through the rooms.

'*Hallo*?' he tried again, unable to control the slight tremor in his voice as his heart rate began to rise. The glow had now gone completely, to be replaced by a chilliness in his bones. He stepped forward, the flags ringing hollowly under his feet. He groped along the wall, seeking a light-switch near the door.

Something crunched under his feet.

Arnold stood still. Slowly he bent down, touched the stone flags, and he felt the slivers, sharp under his fingers. The light-bulb in the passageway had been shattered.

Alarmed, Arnold straightened, and called again. 'Miss Ellis? Miss Sauvage-Brown? Is there anyone here?'

He groped his way down the passageway, not waiting for an answer. Again there came the crunching sound under his feet — another light — bulb. They had been systematically smashed — of that he was now sure.

There was a pounding in Arnold's temples as he tried to recall the layout of the farmhouse. The passageway was cool, but he could feel warmth ahead of him, the kitchen probably, and even as he realized it he caught the dim glow under the door itself.

There was an open fire there: some light at least would be available.

He opened the door and the fire was low, turning to ash, and leaving only a dim light for the kitchen. It was enough for Arnold to see there was little sign of disturbance; a chair had been moved, leaning against the settee. But there was something that bothered Arnold, something that brought back unpleasant, half-recalled memories. An odour, a sickly, cloying odour that seemed to pervade the room.

Arnold swayed. He was drunker than he had realized, and although the tension and the thundering of his heart had sobered him somewhat, he was still left with uncoordinated muscles and muddled thought. He stood in the kitchen and tried to think straight.

A phone. There'd been a phone. Far corner of the room, in the angle of the old farmhouse kitchen. This was no business for him, an empty house with that disturbing smell. Police: he needed to call the police.

He moved towards the angle of the wall and immediately, in the dull glow of the firelight, he saw the huddled shape lying in the corner. He stopped dead, stared at it and recalled the odour and what it meant. Spilled blood.

His senses began to reel. He wanted to extend a hand, touch the body lying there, but he could not nerve himself to do so. His gorge rose, sickness threatening to choke him and, gagging, he stepped over the huddled body, reached for the phone and dialled 999.

He was able to gasp only, 'Police . . . Penbrook Farm,' before the phone dropped from his nerveless fingers and, retching, he staggered back into the centre of the room. He knelt in front of the settee, his stomach heaving, alcohol and distress combining to unman him completely.

His senses began to blur, but before the blackness descended upon him he recalled the police car in the lane, bearing Mildred Sauvage-Brown away from the farm. She had been calling out, triumphant and defiant.

They would never get the farm, she had insisted. Except one way.

Over her dead body.

3

'Just what in the hell were you doing there?'

It was a question that had hammered at Arnold for twenty-four hours. It had first been asked of him when the police had brought him out of the kitchen, still groggy, into the front room as arc lights had been set up and cars had driven up to the farmhouse and there had been much coming and going. Still hazy from his consumption of alcohol he had been almost incoherent and was not surprised when the detective questioning him had expressed doubt about his answers and hinted he suspected the murderer of the woman in the kitchen was Arnold himself.

But everything had changed when Chief Superintendent Fairbairn had walked into the room, for he had brought a woman with him. At the sight of her Arnold had started to his feet as though a bomb had gone off. He cried out choking, pointing an accusatory finger. '*You!*'

Dumpy, angry, shaking with suppressed emotion, Mildred Sauvage-Brown had snarled at him, 'You bastard!'

'But I thought it was you!' Arnold exclaimed, bewildered.

'And you killed her, thinking it was me!' Mildred Sauvage-Brown screamed, struggling to get at Arnold but held back by the Chief Superintendent. Two constables were called in to restrain her. Fairbairn looked at Arnold curiously. 'You thought it was Miss Sauvage-Brown who had been murdered?'

'I never thought of Miss Ellis,' Arnold replied, shaking his head, desperately trying to clear the fogs in his mind. 'The house was dark, the lights had been smashed I wasn't thinking straight, and when I came into the kitchen . . . there was the blood, and the body in the corner and I rang the police . . . and then passed out.'

'*Murderer!*' Mildred Sauvage-Brown hissed.

'Get that bloody woman out of here,' Chief Superintendent Fairbairn snapped, unfeelingly in Arnold's view. She would, after all, be much upset by the death of her companion, and she should be forgiven a degree of anger and passion. Fairbairn had then questioned Arnold closely, but had not got very far. Now, in Fairbairn's own office the following day, the man obviously hoped to get the facts a little straighter.

'I'd been drinking,' Arnold admitted.

'We know that. It was perfectly obvious. You'd been sick either from the drink, or from the sight of Sarah Ellis's corpse, or a combination, didn't matter too much. But why had you gone there?'

'I . . . I got drunk, and decided to have it out with Miss Sauvage-Brown.'

'Have what out?'

'Her . . . attitude.' Arnold was himself puzzled at his answer. The resentments he had felt had now faded; they had been inflamed by alcohol and they now seemed very trivial. He found it difficult to explain to the Chief Superintendent. 'You don't really suspect me of killing Miss Ellis, do you?'

'You're not ruled out,' Fairbairn said grudgingly, 'but there's no real signs you had much to do with it. No scratches, no signs of contact, no blood . . . And your behaviour, well, murderers don't usually ring us after they've croaked someone. Unless they're fiendishly clever. You don't seem to me to be fiendishly clever.'

'Miss Sauvage-Brown seems to think I did it.'

'Last night, she did.' Fairbairn shrugged. 'But this morning she'll have had time to reflect. But tell me — why did you think it was she who'd been killed?'

Arnold frowned. 'I suppose . . . well, it was partly that Miss Ellis was so . . . harmless.'

'Whereas the outspoken Miss Sauvage-Brown has spent most of her adult life making enemies of one sort or another.' The Chief Superintendent nodded. 'Anything else?'

'The words she used when you arrested her earlier. Over her dead body . . .'

'You thought them prophetic.'

'Something like that.'

Fairbairn watched Arnold closely for a little while. 'You puzzle me, Mr Landon. You say you went there to have a confrontation with Miss Sauvage-Brown. She clearly dislikes you — I'm told she attacked you after a planning inquiry recently. Do you so much dislike her?'

Arnold shrugged uncertainly. 'I was drunk—'

'Were you also drunk when you posted bail for her?' Fairbairn interrupted.

'No.'

'Funny thing to do, if you disliked her, wanted to confront her, been attacked by her . . .'

'She's . . . a difficult woman,' Arnold said weakly.

'And you're a funny feller,' Fairbairn said grumpily. 'All right, when you drove to the farm did you see any other cars on the road?'

'I passed a few, but—'

'Did you make out any of them?'

Arnold shook his head. 'Just dazzled by their lights, really.'

'You didn't see a Rover near the farm?'

'No, sir.'

Fairbairn scowled. 'We've had a report of a Rover being driven fast from that area. Complaint from a farmer who was almost knocked down. Like you, he was drunk. Unlike you, he was walking home. You didn't see the car?'

'No.'

'How long were you in the farmhouse before you found the body?'

'I would calculate a matter of minutes only.'

'Can you tell me what time you left your office?'

'About nine, I think.'

'Anyone to verify that?'

'I don't think so.'

'How long did it take you to drive to Penbrook Farm?'

'About an hour, I would calculate.'

Chief Superintendent Fairbairn grunted. 'I have to tell you, Mr Landon, that early reports from forensic would suggest — from body cooling times — that Sarah Ellis was killed close to nine thirty, nine forty-five.'

Arnold stared at the Chief Superintendent, his mouth open. 'You mean . . . it happened only minutes before I got there?'

'Something like that,' Fairbairn said quietly. 'The person who killed her must have wanted to leave the house without being seen. Switching out the lights would have done that, but he — or she — must have panicked, smashed the lightbulbs, so the house could be left in darkness. Another reason for not holding you a *likely* suspect: no sign of glass slivers in your clothes.'

Arnold hesitated. 'How was she killed?'

'She was swung, with considerable violence, against the wall near the fireplace. Her head struck the wall — it crushed her head, lots of blood. She was pushed, or fell, in the corner near the phone.'

'The person who killed her . . . you said he — or she.' Chief Superintendent Fairbairn regarded him blandly. 'We have still an open mind about the sex of the killer. I wonder . . . would you mind if I asked Miss Mildred SauvageBrown to join us at this point?'

* * *

She sat squarely in the chair to one side of Arnold, eyes smouldering dislike, anger and a deeper, more personal emotion that Arnold could not detect but could guess at. Chief Superintendent Fairbairn had called for cups of coffee and they waited for them in silence, the policeman obviously happy to allow the tension to grow between the two people facing him. Mildred Sauvage-Brown's dumpy face sagged at the jowls and there was an unwonted pallor in her cheeks; the hands in her lap were twisted together, and Arnold shivered slightly at the thought she possibly wanted to get her fingers around his throat.

The coffee arrived at last.

Chief Superintendent Fairbairn smiled. 'Sugar?' he asked Miss Sauvage-Brown.

'Three spoons,' she replied balefully and glared at Arnold. 'Are you going to arrest him?'

'What for?' the Chief Superintendent inquired.

'He was there at the farm. What was he doing there? Didn't he kill poor Sarah?'

Arnold looked at his hands. There had been a spasm in the woman's voice, and although it was still bitter it seemed to have lost some of its positive aggression.

Fairbairn handed her the cup of coffee. She took it grudgingly. Fairbairn sipped his own coffee and said, 'There's little or no evidence to connect Mr Landon with the murder, although he seems to have doubtful motives for being there. I thought perhaps you might be able to help.'

'Why the hell should I know why he went to the farm?' she snapped. 'You got him here in your office. Why not ask *him*?'

'I have,' Fairbairn said blandly. 'He says he was there because of you.'

'*Me?*' Arnold's heart sank as Mildred Sauvage-Brown's voice rose in surprise. Her cup clattered on the desk. She glared at Arnold. 'What did I have to do with your going to Penbrook Farm?'

'I . . . I decided to have a word with you,' Arnold said weakly. It had seemed a good idea at the time. Sober, he had reviewed the situation with less confidence.

'About what?'

'Your attitude,' Fairbairn said with a smirk.

'*Attitude?*'

Arnold summoned his strength of mind and purpose. He was unable to meet the fury of her glance but he said, 'I have been . . . concerned about the way you've been behaving.'

'You've been what?'

'You've done the cause of Penbrook Farm no good. You've alienated magistrates, you've drawn bad publicity to yourself, you've behaved in an obstreperous manner and got yourself jailed — in fact, you've shown all the worst characteristics of so-called conservationists who give causes a bad name and as far as I'm concerned—'

'At least I don't go around killing old ladies!' Mildred Sauvage-Brown roared.

The words struck the room to silence. Arnold stared at her, shocked. He was aware of Chief Superintendent Fairbairn waiting behind his desk like a predatory bird, waiting to pounce, but Mildred Sauvage-Brown's face was drained of all colour and her hands were shaking. She had already come to terms with the death of her companion, of that Arnold was sure: Mildred Sauvage-Brown had a tough constitution, physically and emotionally. But it was another thing to handle words like *killing*, and to accuse, face to face, another human being.

Quietly Arnold said, 'I assure you, my presence at Penbrook Farm is accounted for by a drunken desire on my part to tell you what I've just told you now. When I got there, Miss Ellis was dead. I was . . . overcome. The next thing I remember was the arrival of the police.'

'What was the next thing *you* remember, Miss Sauvage-Brown?' Chief Superintendent Fairbairn asked in a silky, innocent tone.

'After what?' she asked, only half-understanding the question

'After leaving the police station, having posted bail for yourself,' Fairbairn purred.

Mildred Sauvage-Brown stared at him, deep glints of anger moving in her eyes. 'What are you trying to say?'

'I'm not *trying* to say anything. Like Mr Landon here, your behaviour is somewhat curious. First of all you seem to want to be shoved in jail; then you change your mind and want to get out. Having got out . . . where did you go?'

'I told you yesterday.'

'Not very satisfactorily. Tell me again.'

She shot a swift glance in Arnold's direction. Reluctantly she said, 'I decided to carry out certain investigations.'

'For what reason?'

'To support allegations I'd made in the courtroom.' Again she looked at Arnold. 'The fact is, after a few hours in the police cells I decided I wouldn't be getting very far. Not that way. I *know* what's been going on behind the purchase of Penbrook Farm, but until I come up with some facts there'll be no chance anyone will do anything about it. So I decided to get out of there. No one else is interested enough, or active enough to do it. I am. So I got out.'

'And . . . ?'

'I made some inquiries.'

Fairbairn smiled. 'About what?'

'About certain business activities here in the North-East.'

'Did you come up with any answers?'

She hesitated. 'I *know* those bastards . . .'

'Any proofs?'

Chief Superintendent Fairbairn was treated to one of Mildred Sauvage-Brown's special glares. He seemed unaffected. 'No proofs,' he declared with satisfaction. 'And no record of where you went or to whom you spoke during this period.'

Mildred Sauvage-Brown's chin came up stubbornly.

Chief Superintendent Fairbairn turned to Arnold. 'The fact is, Mr Landon, we have something odd here. You turn up at the farm and phone us to tell us Miss Ellis is dead. Or something to that effect. Miss Sauvage-Brown does not.'

'I wasn't there.'

'Not at the farm? Not since your release from the cells? Where did you go? You wandered, you say. Made inquiries. Came up with nothing . . . or at least nothing you're prepared or able to divulge to us. No one you can name to say where you've been. Until you happen to be approaching the farm after we got there.'

'I was going home.'

'After Miss Ellis's death.'

'I didn't know—'

'If you *had* been there would it have happened?'

'How can I tell? If I had been there . . .' Her words suddenly died away. She stared, stricken, at the Chief Superintendent, and the colour slowly came back to her face, cheeks becoming ruddy as though she were embarrassed. But it was not embarrassment, Arnold was sure. It was the warmth of anger, the slow surge of fury as realization dawned upon her, overcoming the blackness of her grief and shock at the death of Sarah Ellis. 'Good God,' she said harshly. 'It *was* me!'

'You?'

'It was me . . . *me* who should have been killed. It was me they were after.'

'I hardly think—'

'But it's obvious! The bastard, he'll have heard I was sniffing around. I'd shouted things out in the courtroom and that was bad enough, but when I started making inquiries around the coast, along the river, he heard about it and he went out to that farm and he . . .'

Her words died away again. She sat dumbly, dully, introspective. Fairbairn waited. There was a tight feeling in Arnold's chest. Her lips moved. 'Conspiracy,' she whispered. '*Murder* . . .'

'We're all aware a murder has been committed,' Fairbairn said roughly. 'And your own activities and movements, still unaccounted for, mean that you yourself are not entirely cleared of suspicion. The natural thing would have been for you to go home; you did not, and so . . .'

'But it was me he really meant to kill.'

'A motive—'

'The motive for killing me is obvious. I've been making too much noise,' she said wildly. 'I'm rocking too many boats. They went to the farm—'

'They?'

'That bastard Minford! Wilson maybe, or Livingstone — how the hell do I know? It's your job to work it out, your job to find the proof. I was interfering in their plans and they *conspired*—'

'Have you any proof of this?'

'Proof? Don't talk to me about proof. It's all so damned obvious, can't you see it? Wilson and Livingstone want to buy the farm. The spin-off for council support through Minford is the damned old people's home. The pair of them — Wilson and Livingstone — will get the building contracts in the area thereafter . . . It's so *obvious*.'

'And it leads to murder?'

'I had to be silenced. One of them went there—'

'Can you prove that?'

'You prove it, damn it! You're the bloody copper!'

'And you're a wild theorist who throws out allegations based on no fact!' Fairbairn snapped, reddening.

'I had to be silenced. One of them — Minford, check what he was up to. And Wilson, even though I doubt he'd do it himself. That Livingstone character, he's a hard bastard and I wouldn't trust him further than I could throw him and that's no distance. Yes, Livingstone, he could do it. He's hard, a nasty piece of work behind all that smoothness. Check on him, find out what he was up to—'

'Does he drive a Rover?'

She stared at him, taken aback. 'How the hell do I know?'

'I thought you'd made inquiries.'

'You still suspect *me*?'

Fairbairn glowered. 'I suspect anyone who makes wild unsupported allegations, maybe to cover her own activities, against respectable businessmen—'

'*Respectable?*' Mildred Sauvage-Brown was almost beside herself with fury. 'They're raping the countryside, man. Is that respectable? They're subverting public morality. Is that respectable? They're making secret profits, using the cloak of democratic proceedings to feather their own nests—'

'Miss Sauvage-Brown, you say you've been making inquiries,' Chief Superintendent Fairbairn intervened, and you continue making these wild allegations, but I ask again, do you have any *proofs*?'

'But it's so *obvious*,' Mildred Sauvage-Brown almost screamed at him. 'What do you want? You want a picture of the man killing Sarah? You want a written confession that he thought it was me, that he intended killing me, that he killed her by mistake? You want a photostat record of the shady deals that are behind the whole situation? You want a tape-recording of the conspirators? You want a video show of their nefarious activities?'

'I want proofs, Miss Sauvage-Brown!' Chief Superintendent Fairbairn thundered.

'But can't you see the facts that lie in front of your face? You stupid man, can't you see the whole thing is so circumstantially obvious? Damn it, it's as obvious as a trout in the milk!'

At the look on Chief Superintendent Fairbairn's face Arnold closed his eyes and groaned.

Mentally.

When Miss Sauvage-Brown was led from the room she was still shouting. *'It's as obvious as a trout in the milk!'*

CHAPTER FOUR

1

One of the advantages of having a reputation for a mild eccentricity was that shopkeepers adopted a rather caring attitude towards you, Arnold concluded. They seemed to feel that you were to be protected, cosseted even. In the case of the lady in Morpeth who worked in the cleaning and repair shop, it was a fussiness towards him, in the way she folded the clothes he took for cleaning, and the manner in which she gently chided and admonished him as on this occasion, when he took in his coat for repair. 'I don't know, Mr Landon, what you need is a good woman.' She giggled. 'Or even a bad one. But a woman, any road, who'll look after you proper. Stop you getting yourself into scrapes. Make sure you're home at night when you should be. None of this going with bad companions like that Freddie Keeler. Too much money he has, not enough sense. I bet he had something to do with this tear in your coat!'

Arnold felt unable to disabuse her of her prejudices. He smiled patiently, bobbed his head a little to confirm her opinion of his helplessness and then took his car to the car wash, where the lady behind the desk always demonstrated her own view of his helplessness by actually driving his car through the wash for him. 'I know you don't like doing it,' she said.

'I remember the first time, when you got stuck in there with the window half way down and the brushes shoving water in all over you. Didn't you half come out like a drowned duck!'

Arnold recalled it all too well. It was the reason why he was quite happy to allow her to look after him in this manner.

But there was another advantage to mild eccentricity. It was that one became accepted by people who were mildly eccentric themselves. Arnold's own peculiarity was harmless enough. Unmarried, he liked to live alone and devote his spare time to a study of the hills and ruined villages of the Northumberland hinterland. Stone and wood were his passions: where others saw them as dead, inanimate things, for him they spelled out history, lives, realities far divorced from the modern plastic world. And as his own eccentricity became known over the years, he had been drawn into a small circle of other enthusiasts. They were acquaintances rather than friends because their lives were bound up and circumscribed by their own enthusiasms. They could never become *close*: but they respected one another's feelings, and skills, and most of all, one another's knowledge.

One such was a man who lived in a tumbledown old presbytery in Felton. He had discovered a Victorian rubbish tip in his back garden and had excavated it lovingly for twenty years. His collection of bottles, Victorian bric-a-brac, samplers and irons was probably unique and certainly worth a considerable amount of money, but what was remarkable to Arnold and the rest of the world was the man's intensive knowledge of the minutia: of the period, of the way their ancestors had lived, of what had been *unimportant* in their lives.

Another was Ben Gibson.

He looked like a decrepit frog. He had large, hooded eyes set in a fleshy, squat face. His back was bent, joints crippled by arthritis, so his small stature was rendered even smaller by his crouching gait. He was perhaps seventy years of age and had been a watchmaker until he was forced to close down his small business, from lack of custom and stiffening joints. He lived near Newcastle's Quayside, in the lower ground-floor rooms of a building that had once flourished in the old commercial days on the waterfront but which now echoed mustily to the feet of struggling entrepreneurs, starting new businesses in unsuitable premises, drifting into bankruptcy, and replaced by other, similarly hopeful, hopeless dreamers.

He always drank Earl Grey tea.

Arnold always enjoyed visiting Ben Gibson, not just for the tea he provided. There was a mustiness about the premises that was redolent of another age; he loved the echo in the stairwell when he stood there caressing the old oak balustrades and the whispers came down from the floors above; the light that filtered through the long rectangular windows was softened in its impact, heightening the impression that he had stepped back a hundred years.

And in some respects Ben's enthusiasms touched upon his own.

'Ah, Mr Landon, I'm delighted you've called on me. You'll be more than interested in the fact I've managed to get my hands on a rather battered but still complete copy of de Gheyn's *Croniques et Conquestes de Charlemaine* for, even though it is divorced from your own interests, the copy itself was wrapped in this . . .'

Ben Gibson knew all about Arnold's passions, and he cackled as Arnold handled with reverence the faded material that had once comprised an indenture between two carpenters and a builder.

'Amazing, is it not?' Ben Gibson said, his large frog eyes glowing with pleasure. 'Difficult to read of course. *Soudelet* . . .'

'Or *sondelet*, a saddle-bar,' Arnold offered.

'Yes, exactly, and *vertivel* . . .'

'It's sometimes printed as *vertinel*. It means a hinge-band,' Arnold explained.

'That's the trouble,' Ben Gibson said, rocking gently in his seat by the table as he nourished the thought, 'in most old handwritten manuscripts it's impossible to distinguish between *n, u* and *v*. It's only by tracing variant spellings that you can reach certainty.'

'There's also the point that the clerks who wrote these documents were liable to slips of the pen, naturally; and sometimes they were putting on parchment purely local terms of which they could give, at best, only a phonetic rendering.'

'Fascinating.'

'An interesting find.'

'One lives for such moments. More tea, Mr Landon?' Arnold took some more Earl Grey tea. He sat quietly for a little while as Ben Gibson enthused over his find, and over his copy of de Gheyn. The man was entitled to his triumph and Arnold could understand the thrill that would be running through the old man's arthritic bones as he talked about it. He also knew that Gibson would, in a little while, recall his duty as a host, and make polite inquiry of Arnold's own interests.

'I see you've been in the news again,' the little man said with a sly grin, at last. 'I'm sure your superior officer will be getting nervous.'

Ben Gibson knew all about the Senior Planning Officer. Arnold sighed and nodded. 'He's due back next week. I'm pretty certain there'll be some harsh words.'

'But you'll have had the satisfaction of finding something interesting out at the farm you visited?'

Arnold nodded. 'Some mediaeval tile work. But it's not that I've come to see you about. I'm aware of your deep knowledge of old manuscripts and papers of any antiquity. I've picked up something I'd like you to have a look at.'

The little man's eyes glowed again with interest. Arnold unzipped the leather file case he had placed on the table between them and extracted the folder. Inside the folder was a single sheet of paper. In the filtered light of the room the colour of the initial letters seemed faded and tired, but the print itself, and the Latin words, were clear enough. Ben Gibson took the folder, not touching the sheet, and he peered at it, inspected it closely, his lips soundlessly mouthing the words it contained.

'It's been treated roughly. There are stains . . . and dirt at the edges.' There was a hint of accusation in Ben Gibson's tone. 'The lower edge is torn.'

Arnold nodded. 'I'm afraid that might be my fault.'

'What's the provenance of the sheet?'

'I don't know.'

Ben Gibson raised his head, gazed almost accusingly at Arnold for a few seconds, before lowering his eyes to the sheet again, caressing the words with his glance, shaking his head slightly from side to side as he read. 'So where did you come across it, then?'

'I'm not sure.'

There was a short silence. Ben Gibson raised his head again, staring at Arnold, and then carefully put down the folder. 'I don't understand.'

Arnold shrugged helplessly. 'You must appreciate I live alone, and I collect all sorts of bits and pieces of paper, some connected with my interests, some not — ephemera, really, like articles in journals on architecture, that sort of thing.'

'Well?'

'Every so often I decide to have a clear out. The return of the Senior Planning Officer,' Arnold said sheepishly, 'affects me in a curious way. I take the car to the car wash; I clean it out; I get my clothes repaired; I empty the wastepaper baskets; I get together all the accumulation of paper in the house and give the place a spring clean . . . I know it's nothing to do with the Senior Planning Officer, I mean he's never been to my bungalow, but I feel it necessary. *Compulsive*.'

Ben Gibson regarded him gravely. He touched the folder gently. 'And?'

'And I went out to the bin in the back yard,' Arnold said, 'and I tipped the rubbish out and just as I was turning away I caught a glimpse of the Latin. I drew the sheet out—'

'Out of the *dustbin*?'

Shamefaced, Arnold nodded. 'I've no idea how it got there. I will have had it somewhere in the house, unwittingly. But once I saw it, inspected it . . . do you know what it is?'

Ben Gibson continued to stare at him thoughtfully for a full half-minute. Then his glance returned to the sheet. He shook his head in a slow doubt. 'I'm not sure. I can tell you it has a certain . . . antiquity. Its provenance . . . I'm not sure. I will need to check certain references, undertake some inquiries. Are you prepared to leave it with me, Mr Landon?'

'Of course.'

'Even if it is valuable?'

'Is it?'

'To me,' Ben Gibson said quietly, 'and men like me. To others, possibly not. But enthusiasts . . . they are sometimes unscrupulous.'

Arnold Landon smiled. 'Not true enthusiasts. I trust you, Mr Gibson. Besides, I brought it here out of interest, to see what it is. It's not my field. Once I know what it is I shall be happy to make a gift of it to you.'

'Perhaps not, Mr Landon, perhaps not.' Obviously pleased at the thought, the little man nevertheless seemed still a little concerned. 'One matter I would ask of you. Please consider again, try to think where you might have been keeping this sheet. I would certainly be interested to discover its provenance.'

'I'll do what I can,' Arnold promised.

* * *

He made a start that very evening. He began in his study upstairs. It was about time he started trying to bring order to the collection of papers, magazines, journals, books, maps and commentaries he had collected there over the years. The trouble was, once he started sifting through the material he quickly discovered that there was so much there he had intended to read but had not got around to reading that it was bedtime before he had even dented the surface of the problem.

It was going to be a long job, even if he disciplined himself not to follow every little interesting track disclosed as he turned over papers and books. He had to be systematic. He started to arrange the books in piles, and proceeded to leaf through them, carefully.

The following day he had to spend most of his time at a public inquiry in Morpeth. For much of the day he was barely occupied and was given the opportunity to let his thoughts wander, as the public inspector droned on in the report of his findings. Arnold's thoughts turned to Mildred Sauvage-Brown and her over-excitability. And what on earth was it she had shouted in Chief Superintendent Fairbairn's office?

A trout in the milk.

Curious. Arnold had no idea what she could possibly have meant.

It was still on his mind when the hearing was adjourned.

He glanced at his watch: there was no need to return to the planning office and the library did not close until seven. He left his car where it was and walked across to the public library, entered the reference room and found a dictionary of quotations.

Oddly enough, he found it quickly, even though it was not a quotation familiar to him. Thoreau. *Some circumstantial evidence is very strong, as when you find a trout in the milk.*

What could Mildred Sauvage-Brown be trying to say in that context?

* * *

He spent another long evening looking through his books in the study. It was a fruitless search. There was another block of books on the shelves in the sitting-room but he felt too weary to go through them. They could wait until the following day.

Next morning he dealt with outstanding papers that needed to be cleared before the Senior Planning Officer returned from Scarborough. One of them was the matter of Willington Hall. He had read in the newspaper that the funeral of Patrick Willington was to take place; now, he was able to close the matter of the planning application for the sawmill at the Hall.

He wondered vaguely how Henry Willington would cope. The man had seemed dazed, uncoordinated in a sense, shaken by the death of his father and by the enormity of the task facing him, even if it was something he had been waiting to undertake for years.

Previously, Henry had been able to blame Patrick Willington for the failure of the Willington estate. In future, he alone would have to bear the responsibility.

And, perhaps, the disappointing reality of knowing that Willington Hall could not be saved.

Arnold had a headache when he went home. For a while, after he had eaten a frugal meal of tuna fish and salad, he thought of simply watching television for the evening. Then he remembered the glow in Ben Gibson's eyes and decided he should carry on with his search.

At eight thirty he was surrounded by a pile of books on the sitting-room floor, patiently working through each one, when the bell to the front door rang.

Arnold sat up on his heels, puzzled. He rarely had visitors at his bungalow, and never in the evening. There were no friends to call, no close relatives. Occasionally the newspaper boy called for his payment; once a month the milkman called. Frowning, Arnold went to the front door, switched on the porch light, and made out the vague form of one person, indistinguishable through the frosted glass of the door.

Cautiously Arnold opened the door.

It was Mildred Sauvage-Brown.

* * *

She stood squinting at him uncertainly, her pouched eyes screwed up with doubt. She was wearing a dark overcoat, with a black band on the arm, sewed clumsily above the elbow. The folds in her face seemed to have sagged and her shoulders had lost their aggression: vulnerability seemed to have crept into her bearing and this woman was a long way distant from the one who had thrust a shotgun muzzle into Arnold's face at Penbrook Farm.

'Miss Sauvage-Brown!'

She had difficulty responding. She looked around her as though questioning her own presence; glanced at the sky as though sniffing the wind. She could not meet his glance, and she shuffled, her boots scuffing the stone and making a scraping sound.

Arnold cleared his throat. 'Can I . . . help you?'

She shot one quick glance at him and it was as full of pride as ever; then the uncertainty came again and she frowned, still saying nothing. Arnold stepped back. 'Perhaps you'd better come in.'

It was possible she detected the hesitancy in his tone, for she herself hesitated. He waited, and she made up her mind, ducking in an odd fashion as she entered the bungalow as though she expected to bang her head on the ceiling. Arnold led the way into the sitting-room. She stared at the piles of books.

'I'm sorry about the mess,' Arnold said inadequately. She hardly seemed to hear him. She stared at the books without speaking and as the silence lengthened between them Arnold said nervously, 'Would you care for a glass of sherry?'

She started slightly and nodded. Arnold turned away thankful that at last she was responding in some way, and he poured two glasses of medium sherry. There was no choice; he catered only for his own tastes. When he turned round she was sitting down, the coat loosened at her throat.

'Thank you,' she said as he handed her the glass of sherry. 'You think I'm crazy, don't you?'

Arnold stared at her. 'I've never said that.'

'No. In your typically *British* way you'd understate it. You'd call me *overenthusiastic*, or something like that.'

'Perhaps something like that,' Arnold agreed.

'Humph,' she said and sipped her sherry. It seemed to relax her somewhat, bring some confidence, the old aggressiveness back into her veins. 'You think I'm wrong, too, don't you?'

'About what?'

'Everything.'

'No. Not about the farm. You have a case . . . you had a case with which I'm in sympathy. I just felt . . .'

'That I went the wrong way about getting it put right.' The pouched eyes glittered suddenly. 'And you think I'm wrong about the rest of it?'

'The rest of it . . .' Arnold shrugged. 'You've made so many accusations . . . unbacked by facts . . . What did you mean by that trout in the milk remark?'

Contemptuously she said, 'You didn't get it?'

'No.'

'What's the natural habitat of the trout?'

'Water, of course.'

'So if you find a trout in the milk, it's circumstantial evidence that the bloody milk's been watered, isn't it?' she demanded. Gloomily she added, 'They used to do quite a bit of that in the old days. Watering milk to make it go further. Helped the spread of cholera.'

'I still don't understand the significance of the remark, as far as we're concerned,' Arnold ventured.

'Oh, I can't produce *evidence* of Minford's involvement in the shenanigans behind the Penbrook Farm deal, not the kind Fairbairn would call for. I tried hard enough, while Sarah . . . I tried hard enough, but I can't produce it, but damn it, Landon, the *facts* are there, the *circumstances*, and if the bloody police would only probe them, draw the conclusions from that circumstantial evidence . . .' She paused and eyed him warily, almost grumpily. 'You tried to go bail for me.'

Arnold sipped his sherry nervously.

'You tried to go bail for me and I wouldn't have it,' she insisted. 'Why did you do that? You don't even like me.'

'There were . . . circumstances . . . situations . . .'

'What?'

'I . . . I got angry.'

Her little eyes grew eager with interest. 'Angry? Because you guessed maybe I was right after all?'

'No. It wasn't like that. I . . . I'd been talking to some people. They reminded me, triggered something in my mind, and I checked.'

'What did you find?' Mildred Sauvage-Brown asked.

Arnold took a deep breath. 'A few years ago there was a company called Jarrow Development Corporation. It was run by a man called Floyd. He had a daughter called Eileen. She married a man called Simson, and they had a son.'

'So?'

'Simson died, Eileen Simson was widowed and her father's business began to run into problems. It was eventually the subject of a merger with a company run by Albert Minford's father.'

Mildred Sauvage-Brown straightened in her chair. 'Go on; this is getting interesting.'

Arnold shook his head. 'Don't read too much into all this. What happened was that the merger never really worked and the company was closed down, albeit leaving Albert Minford with a fair amount of money, enough to enable him to enter politics and make a living out of it.'

Mildred Sauvage-Brown growled something under her breath.

'In the meanwhile,' Arnold continued, 'Albert Minford and Eileen Simson decided to get married. With her husband in local politics and at a loose end, I suppose it was natural that she should go back to the kind of background she knew. She set up a building firm with her son: she used her maiden name in doing so, perhaps to make use of old contacts and goodwill, with her son coming in as a codirector in his own name. Floyd and Simson.'

The pouched eyes glittered. 'That's not the end of it.'

Arnold shrugged. 'The company has won a few local authority building contracts.'

'With Albert Minford pulling the strings.'

'There's no evidence of that,' Arnold said hurriedly. 'He had no interest to declare because he has no shares in the firm. He wasn't on the committee awarding the contracts. The agreements themselves were all the subject of appropriate tendering procedures and there's nothing there that can be raised in a court of law.'

'But Minford could have been pulling strings, doing the old boy thing, using a network of political friends to swing contracts, disclose tenders, all that sort of petty corruption.'

'There's no evidence of that,' Arnold insisted.

'*But you went bail for me!*'

Arnold took a deep breath. He finished his sherry. He wished there was some whisky in the bungalow. He poured himself another sherry, quite forgetting to offer one to Mildred Sauvage-Brown. 'I . . . I was shaken . . . upset. It was done on the spur of the moment.'

Mildred Sauvage-Brown shook her head. 'That doesn't explain such a committed action.'

'There is no real explanation. It was . . . a reaction.'

'No. You went bail for me for a very good reason. You knew I was right.'

'Miss Sauvage-Brown—'

'You knew I was right; knew what I said about that bastard Minford was true.'

'No.'

'You did it because you knew there was a financial fiddle going on behind the scenes.'

'*No!*'

Her eyes glittered triumphantly. 'You did it because—'

'No!' Arnold said desperately. 'I did it . . . I did it because I felt sorry for you.'

The words were out before he could stop them. The impact was immediate upon Mildred Sauvage-Brown. For several seconds she stared at him, bewildered, open-mouthed in astonishment. Slowly, her expression changed. The excitement, the flush of triumph that had been flooding her cheeks as she thought Arnold was on her side was fading. It was replaced by something else, a compound of puzzlement and embarrassment, disbelief and resistance. Then that too began to fade as she paled, her mouth tightening, her eyes slitting angrily. She looked away, glared at the empty sherry glass in her hand. Silence grew between them, painfully; her hand was shaking with suppressed tension. Arnold wished the words back; wished the earth would swallow him.

Mildred Sauvage-Brown looked up. Her glance was cold as death and as unrelenting. 'Don't ever say that to me again, Mr Landon.'

Arnold opened his mouth, but no words came. He had insulted her, shamed her, touched her at her most vulnerable point. She had built her character upon independence, and she was unable to accept that she should rely on sympathy, or kindness, from a man. She had refused the bail he had tendered. He understood why.

Silently he took the glass from her hand and poured her another drink. His hand was trembling slightly; she appeared not to notice as she took the glass from him. The atmosphere in the room was still tense; she turned away from him, and looked about her. 'Spring cleaning,' she said.

Arnold took a deep breath, aware the moment was easing.

'Not really spring cleaning. I'm just looking for something.'

'It's a mess.'

He agreed with the uncompromising statement. 'Yes.'

There was a short silence, and she relented somewhat. 'Much the same at Penbrook Farm. Nothing seems quite the same since . . . Things out of place. I'm . . . disorientated.'

'I can understand that.'

'Can you?' She shot a wary glance in his direction, still smarting. Arnold waited, and after a while she relaxed a little again. 'I came north for good reason,' she said.

'So I believe.'

'I knew little about the area. Oh, I'd read the romantic stuff about marauding Danes in the twelfth century, burned abbeys, plundered churches, the ever-present threat of the longships. And I saw the trickle of the new invaders, the different breed who merely plunder the silence of the dunes of Lindisfarne, the people who just want to see the pele towers, take a boat to watch the Farne lights blinking in the dusk, listen to *Johnnie Armstrong* played on the Northumbrian pipes. They are harmless . . . a nuisance perhaps to locals who don't need them for a living, but harmless generally. You know what I mean?'

'I do.'

'I didn't come up here looking for trouble,' she said doggedly. 'But when I saw it, I had to act. I could see the other, faceless men, the rape of the countryside, the destruction of a heritage . . . so many people won't *act*, Mr Landon. I *have* to.'

'I understand.'

'Then I met Sarah, and we settled at Penbrook Farm. She was such a gentle person, Mr Landon, she wouldn't harm anyone. And now, I think that if I'd been a different sort of person, if I hadn't been . . . what I am . . . Sarah would still be alive . . .'

She stared dully at the piled books on the carpet. 'You live alone, Mr Landon?'

'Yes.'

'You're used to it.'

'It's the way I like to live.' He managed a short laugh. 'Middle-aged bachelors are difficult people.'

'Middle-aged spinsters too. Perhaps more so. But I haven't lived alone for a long time. It'll take getting used to.' Her voice trembled slightly. 'I'm not sure how I'll manage.'

Arnold did not know what to say. He wanted to sympathize, extend condolences, but she had already rebuffed him when he had crassly suggested he had felt sorry for her. She had pride; she would not welcome any remark that was patronizing. It was a verbal tightrope Arnold was not prepared to walk.

'I've been going through her things,' Mildred Sauvage-Brown said almost dreamily, half-forgetting he was there,

Arnold suspected. 'It's a strange thing. You live with someone for years and you think you know them, understand them, but then . . . it's a surprise. In her trunk, upstairs in the attic of the farmhouse, I found a bundle of letters. I didn't like to read them, but she had no one in the world, so in the end I looked at them. They were sad. She must have been a pretty little thing when she was young. And there was a young man.'

Arnold stood silently, hardly breathing, conscious he was intruding into a private world where Mildred Sauvage-Brown was temporarily lost.

'They were in love. The letters described his feelings. It was beautiful. He wanted to marry her. Something happened. The letters ceased abruptly. There was a lock of hair there — light brown, soft. Clearly, Sarah loved that young man and someone cruelly came between them. It must have been before she wandered in Europe for there were cards, addresses in Italy and Holland. Poor Sarah . . .'

Mildred Sauvage-Brown was silent for a while, lost in thought, staring at the books littering the room. 'She left a will. Two wills, in fact. One was made, oh, twenty years ago. The second a couple of years ago. I'm her beneficiary, taking all her estate.' She stopped, and turned her head suddenly, as though remembering Arnold was there. 'I suppose some people might see that as a motive for murder — for me to murder her, wouldn't they?'

'I hardly believe so,' Arnold murmured.

'Poor Sarah. She's left me everything. I'll have to get probate but I've never needed money. And now . . . Two wills . . . Funny thing, that. The wills were made in different names.'

'How do you mean?'

Mildred Sauvage-Brown frowned. 'The second will, the one in my favour, was made in her own name: Sarah Ellis. But the earlier will, made twenty years ago, that was made in the name of Sarah *Willis*.'

'Was it properly drawn?'

'By a solicitor. And she signed it Sarah Willis. Left all she had to charity.'

'Perhaps she married, in spite of her early experience. Someone called Willis.'

Mildred Sauvage-Brown shook her head. 'No. She told me she'd never married. And the first will, it was drawn up in old form, spinster of this parish, all that sort of stuff. Not that it matters now. Not that any of it matters.'

'You'll miss her.'

Mildred Sauvage-Brown nodded her head and sniffed. Arnold guessed she was near to tears. Perhaps his thought was in some way communicated to her, for suddenly her back stiffened and she snapped, 'Of course I'll miss her. What a bloody silly thing to say.'

'Yes,' Arnold said awkwardly. 'I'm sorry.'

She sniffed again, finished her sherry and contemplated the books on the carpet. 'You've got a lot of clearing up to do there,' she said gloomily.

'It won't take me too long.'

'Humph,' she said, and sat there with her back to him. He could see her face in half-profile and the dumpy, sagging features seemed lost in thought. But the mouth was tightening again, and he gained the impression that her back was straightening, resolution returning to her after the last, embarrassing few minutes when she had exposed her emotions to him, declared her grief at the loss of her companion, and displayed the vulnerability that he would not at one time have guessed lay behind her determined exterior. She stood up abruptly, setting down the glass.

She turned to face him, but she did not see him. He had the odd feeling that she had, indeed, forgotten where she was, or why she was here. She had come to get the answer to a question, and to have contact with a human being who had at least some sympathy with what drove her, and with whom she had in these last days become bound. Now, something else had happened to draw her away, bring back determination to her jaw, recall the glitter of her pouched eyes.

She walked past him, unseeingly. At the front door she paused, recalling old veneers that had not entirely deserted her. 'Thank you for the sherry, Mr Landon,' she said formally. But the glitter was still in her eyes, and the determination had a hint of angry excitement about it.

Arnold opened the door and she stepped out to the drive. There was a drizzle of rain in the air and Mildred SauvageBrown hesitated for a moment, some of her newfound commitment draining from her, perhaps at the darkness of the night, perhaps at its loneliness. She turned, and looked at Arnold. He could not see her eyes.

'Mr Landon . . .' She hesitated, perhaps startled at the plea that lay in her tone. She tested it, measured it against her own personality, and discarded it. The moment was gone.

She walked away, a dumpy, unattractive woman with an ungainly gait, missing the friend and companion of years, and the lump in Arnold's chest was leaden.

2

The return of the Senior Planning Officer from Scarborough was not an occasion for trumpets, eagles and the brazen neighing of warhorses, Arnold thought, but there was certainly an *atmosphere* in the office that morning. He felt the tingle of expectation the moment he entered the building and he remained sensitive, on tenterhooks, until the moment when he was called into the Presence. The sensitivity then moved to his bowels.

The tirade that was visited upon Arnold was in the spirit of what the Senior Planning Officer called a 'roasting'. There were adjectives used that were only vaguely familiar to Arnold, and in general, he conceded privately, the language was colourful and forceful, very much to the point.

The point being that the Senior Planning Officer was more than a little disturbed.

'I have made it clear, Mr Landon,' he finally summed up when he had regained control of his temper, 'and on more than one occasion, that this is a planning office where I expect levels of professionalism and objectivity — where we retain a distance from our clients and our political masters, where we do not get involved and where we stay out of scandalous and damaging situations. You have, over the last couple of years failed to maintain the standards we demand.'

A regal turn of phrase, Arnold considered, that reflected the Senior Planning Officer's view of his own position.

'This, then, is a final warning.' The Senior Planning Officer puffed out his cheeks importantly. 'If you cannot curb the excesses of your enthusiasms and keep your head below the parapet of sensationalism, there is no place for you here in this office. You will be transferred.' His eyes glittered with portents of doom. '*Or worse.*'

He asked Arnold if he understood. Arnold admitted that he did and, much chastened, went back to his desk. He was summoned to the Senior Planning Officer's room again later that afternoon.

They were already seated around the miniature boardroom table that the Senior Planning Officer kept for occasions such as these. The Senior Planning Officer suggested that Arnold already knew everyone present. He did.

Councillor Albert Minford sat at the Senior Planning Officer's left. He was in his usual uniform of neat grey and his eyes were as watchful as ever. His arm was draped carelessly over the back of the chair and he seemed at ease, but there was an inner tension in his body that was barely concealed.

Beside him was the building developer Wilson. He sat squarely in his seat, hands clasped over his spreading belly. He observed Arnold's entry with a mild curiosity, as though recent events had aroused a little more interest in him than he had previously considered possible, but the glance was still cold in its appraisal, and swift in its dismissiveness once again. Wilson was not a man who dealt with petty officials: he even resented the necessity to visit the Senior Planning Officer.

The visit had probably been at the suggestion of his colleague Livingstone. Arnold inspected the man more carefully now, after the comments made about him by Freddie Keeler. Maybe the man would like the sound of crunching bone: the ascetic look about his face was belied by the athleticism of his shoulders, and Arnold could easily imagine the man in a Byker rough-house, down by the river. It was likely his background had been left far behind him since his association with Wilson, but there were still hints of madness in his eyes, the kind of explosive promises that would be activated in the right kind of circumstances.

'I thought it would be useful if you were involved in these discussions, Arnold,' the Senior Planning Officer said coolly, 'since you stood in for me at the planning inquiry. At which, I understand, Miss Sauvage-Brown behaved so reprehensively.'

Wilson shot an impatient glance at the Senior Planning Officer. 'Do you think we can get on?'

'Of course, Mr Wilson. The fact is, gentlemen, the . . . ah . . . demise of Miss Ellis would seem to raise certain problems.'

'Such as?' Livingstone asked.

'Well, clearly, since she was a major objector to the scheme, her . . . removal from the scene may well mean that the proceedings could be delayed.'

'I don't see why,' Livingstone said. His glance slipped towards Arnold and away again. 'She was a major objector but she's dead. I would have thought that meant the opposition would crumble anyway, and there would be no need for a continuation of the inquiry.'

'Things don't quite work like that,' the Senior Planning Officer demurred.

'It's important they *do* work like that,' Livingstone said softly, but behind the softness there was a cutting edge. He half-turned, to look at Albert Minford. 'There's been a considerable amount of effort, and . . . consideration gone into the planning of this scheme. I wouldn't want to see it go awry now. Time is of the essence as far as we are concerned. If we are to proceed, we need to go ahead as quickly as possible.'

Albert Minford cleared his throat. He frowned slightly, staring at the table in front of him, and then he said, 'I see Mr Livingstone's point. I'm in agreement with it. The death of Sarah Ellis is . . . sad, but it's really beside the point. It has no relevance to or bearing on the proceedings, and I feel we should get on with the matter immediately. The necessary orders should go out from this office at once.'

'Mr Sedleigh-Harmon—'

'Arthur Sedleigh-Harmon, QC,' Livingstone interrupted cuttingly, 'has given us an opinion. He feels we should act with despatch.'

'The Chairman—'

'Dick Lansbury.' It was Albert Minford who interrupted the Senior Planning Officer this time. 'He's a politician. He is aware of the pressing needs of this project. He will take the necessary steps.'

Arnold felt warm suddenly. 'By bowing to pressure?' he asked.

Albert Minford's glance was hostile. 'What's that supposed to mean?'

'It would seem to me that you're suggesting political pressure can be brought on Mr Lansbury so that the matter is dealt with quickly, in spite of the interests of the opposing parties.'

Minford's lips grew thin. 'I made no such suggestion. Dick Lansbury is a servant of the community. He will do what he thinks is right. I merely state I think I know how he'll react to the situation. The main opposer is dead. The project is of benefit to the community.'

'There are others—'

'Mildred Sauvage-Brown?' Livingstone queried. He twisted in his chair impatiently. 'The woman's a nut-case. She needs locking up.'

'*Kill* one. *Lock* the other up?'

Arnold's words turned the room to silence. All four men stared at him, the Senior Planning Officer's eyes widening nervously, the other three seemingly turned to stone momentarily. It was Livingstone who found his tongue first. 'Mr Landon,' he said softly, 'you have a loose mouth.'

Hurriedly the Senior Planning Officer interposed. 'Oh, I'm sure Mr Landon didn't mean—'

'What *did* he mean?' Wilson snapped, unclasping his hands and turning them into fists on the table.

'I wasn't implying anything,' Arnold replied. 'I was stating facts. One member of the opposition is killed. A suggestion that the other should be locked up to prevent further opposition—'

'It was a turn of phrase,' Minford said warningly. 'It wasn't a serious proposal.'

'It's just as well,' Arnold said. 'Because any action against Miss Sauvage-Brown would certainly cause eyebrows to be raised, in the circumstances.'

'What circumstances?'

They continued to stare at Arnold as he hesitated in the silence. He shrugged at last. 'Sarah Ellis's will,' he offered.

'Her *will?*' Albert Minford straightened in his seat, relinquishing the relaxed pose he had adopted. 'What about her will?'

'It leaves everything to Miss Sauvage-Brown. Including Penbrook Farm.'

'*The hell it does!*' Livingstone exploded.

The Senior Planning Officer stared thoughtfully at Arnold. 'How do you know this? It's too early for probate to have been granted.'

Uneasily Arnold admitted, 'She told me about it.'

'Who did?'

'Mildred Sauvage-Brown.'

Again there was a short silence. Wilson shifted ponderously in his chair and addressed the Senior Planning Officer. 'Your colleague seems to make odd friendships.'

'Arnold?'

'She's not a friend,' Arnold insisted. 'And I have no real connection with her. I don't even like her . . . But she . . . she's lonely after the death of her companion. She visited me. She told me about the will. And that leaves you with a problem, sir. I'm certain she'll fight tooth and nail to prevent the scheme going through, the more so now that Penbrook Farm is willed to her. She might even see it as a . . . monument to Sarah. She could be very . . . awkward.'

'You can bloody well say that again,' Livingstone said angrily. 'That damned woman's got to be stopped!'

Arnold looked at him curiously. 'I don't quite understand the *urgency* of all this. The situation is more than a little delicate. A police investigation going on into the murder at Penbrook Farm; probate of the will; and Miss Sauvage-Brown's personal views, as the new owner of the farm, about the scheme for development. I can't see that Mr Lansbury will want to hurry through the proposal . . .'

'Mr Bloody Lansbury!' Livingstone snarled. There were flecks of blood in his eyes, and he seemed to be losing control rapidly. 'He'll do what's right, and it's right to get this thing going!'

'Why?' Arnold asked.

The Senior Planning Officer shifted uneasily in his chair but it was Albert Minford who answered. 'You must accept, Mr Landon, that I have some experience of these matters, as a result of my background in the building industry, even though I left it for local politics some years ago. Matters such as the development scheme for Penbrook Farm cannot be set up overnight. They require a great deal of planning as I'm sure you'll be aware. Planning, scheduling, financing—'

'A lot of money can get locked up,' Wilson interrupted.

'Investments are made,' Livingstone said, 'and people expect a rate of return. If they don't get it, problems arise. Cash flow—'

'Charges on land, development costs—'

Albert Minford cleared his throat noisily. It was a warning. Wilson looked at his fists. Livingstone tried to relax, wash the tension from his veins as he still glared at Arnold. 'The fact is,' Minford said, 'delays of this kind cost money. Cost the business money. Cost the ratepayer money. So we have to find ways to . . . expedite matters.'

'There'll be talk,' Arnold advised. 'The Minford Twilight Home. Parcels of land for development beyond the mediaeval woodland.'

'All agreed, with proper notices served,' Minford said smoothly.

'There'll be talk of corruption.'

'Nothing of the kind. All interests have been declared,' Minford insisted. 'And the business deals were agreed after suitable tenders were made.'

'There'll be suggestions that the whole thing must be seen against a wider background. Your wife's firm, Mr Minford. The Amble marina—'

A slow flush stained Minford's features. 'Wild words from Mildred Sauvage-Brown don't make cases, Mr Landon. You'd be well advised not to repeat them.'

'Mr Landon is only trying to . . . advise,' the Senior Planning Officer interrupted hastily.

'His *advice*,' Minford demurred cuttingly, 'seems a trifle biased.'

Silence fell, uneasily. The two businessmen and the councillor avoided each other's eyes; they stared at the Senior Planning Officer as though he held some key to the whole situation. His skin was suddenly sallow, his eyes shadowed with nervousness. He wriggled slightly in his seat, and coughed drily. 'I think . . .' He struggled with the thought. 'I think it'll be best . . . in the circumstances . . . Arnold, thank you for coming in. I'm grateful for your advice. We all are. I think now you've filled me in I can take the matter on from here.'

He was being dismissed. Arnold rose. He was vaguely relieved. It meant he need take no further concern in the matters of Penbrook Farm and the loneliness of Mildred Sauvage-Brown.

* * *

The conference between Livingstone, Wilson, Minford and the Senior Planning Officer went on for some time. Arnold tried to concentrate on the papers on his desk but his mind kept wandering away. There had been an odd atmosphere in the Senior Planning Officer's room: if he didn't know otherwise he would have described it as conspiratorial. The thought unsettled him, and edgily he left his desk and walked through the building until he found himself in the section used by the Department of Administration. Beyond the shelves of steel burdened with law reports he saw the shaggy head of Ned Keeton, bent over a heavy book on the desk.

'Ned?'

'Arnold! Can't keep away these days, hey? After my job? Fed up with the Senior Planning Officer?'

Arnold shrugged noncommittally. 'You busy?'

'Not enough to stop for a cup of tea. Sugar?'

'No, thanks.'

Arnold watched while the lawyer reached under the desk for the illegal kettle. Tea and coffee were served twice a day, and always available from the machines in the corridors, but Ned Keeton had long ago displayed his bloody-mindedness in face of authority and though there had been remonstrations from the Town Clerk, and later the Chief Executive, Ned had blithely ignored them and made his own tea, steaming the room occasionally when he was absent for a while as the kettle boiled on.

The two men sat silently, watching the kettle with a satisfied feeling. It was occasionally pleasant to feel one was bucking the system. When the kettle boiled, Ned Keeton produced a battered teapot from his desk, and made some tea. The mugs were ancient and chipped: Arnold didn't mind. His bore the legend *Lawyers are always appealing.*

'So,' Ned Keeton grunted. 'What's new?'

'Nothing much.'

'Rubbish. Two trips up here in a week or so when otherwise we wouldn't see you twice a year? Something's got on your tits.'

Arnold winced. 'I don't know . . .'

'You know. You want to tell me. Drink up.'

Arnold drank up.

'So now tell me.'

'Nothing I can put my finger on, Ned. Uneasy feeling, that's all.'

'This murder business? I bet the Senior Planning Officer is hopping. Doesn't like publicity.'

'Oh, it's that, of course, but there's something more. He always tells me we've got to be objective, but . . .'

'Well?'

'He's got a meeting with the developers and Councillor Minford. He seems inclined . . . to hurry through the inquiry. And I don't think that's right, Ned.'

'What's to stop it now the old lady's dead?'

'Mildred Sauvage-Brown.'

'She'll have no *locus standi*,' Ned Keeton said. 'Won't classify as an aggrieved person under the statutes.'

'She will if she's the owner. And she's going to be under Sarah Ellis's will.'

'Hah! So that's the situation.' Keeton scratched at his shaggy, greying thatch. 'Interesting. She could certainly oppose then, drag the whole thing out.'

'That's it. The developers want to move quickly. Maybe if they can settle matters before Mildred Sauvage-Brown gets probate . . .'

'Won't serve.' Ned Keeton frowned. 'A will speaks from death, as they say, and that means ownership will hark back — once the will is proved — to the moment of Sarah Ellis's death. No, if they want to hurry things . . . Remind me, these developers . . .'

'Wilson and Livingstone. Councillor Minford's backing them.'

'Oh aye, that bastard.' Keeton thrust out his lower lip thoughtfully. 'Wilson . . . Livingstone . . . Ah now, what was that last week . . . ?'

Arnold sipped his tea while Keeton rummaged through the papers on his desk and then prowled impatiently among the shelves. Twice he struck himself on the forehead with the heel of his hand as though trying to beat memory back into his skull, but when he finally sat down again it was with an air of frustration. 'Time I retired, long past time, I tell you, kiddar. When your memory goes . . . Wilson, and Livingstone, one of them or both of them? They're major shareholders in Aspern International, the European trading firm. Bought in cheap.'

'So?'

'It's going down the tubes, man,' Keeton said blandly. 'It's the report I was looking for, can't bloody find. There's been an investigation, auditors called in, share-dealing frozen, listing suspended, and I'm damned sure those two characters you mention were reported in the *Journal* some time back as having pumped money in considerable quantities into Aspern.'

'I'm not sure I understand.'

'Simple, man. They got a cash flow problem. No wonder they want to get this Penbrook Farm development under way. They'll have investments tied up in Aspern. Their bankers will be getting shirty. They need to show in their business plans a definite, uncluttered proposal to turn around lucrative business — delays are the last thing they'll want to contemplate.'

'You sure about this?'

'Sure?' Ned Keeton squinted up at Arnold. 'Sure enough. I tell you, if I was in their position financially I'd dump my own granny in the Tyne if she had a decent life insurance on her, man!'

Or maybe remove an old lady who stood in their way, by battering her to death in her own farm kitchen.

* * *

It was preposterous. It did not bear thinking about. But Arnold thought about it and could not expunge the picture from his mind when he got back to his office. The girl who worked partly as his secretary — he shared her with another planning officer — told him there had been a phone call for him while he had been with Ned Keeton, and he really should tell her where he was going to be in the building if she was to work efficiently. He took the number from her, and the request to phone back, but he barely noted it. His mind was full of other things.

Was it really conceivable that the financial pressures that Ned Keeton suggested were faced by Wilson and Livingstone would have led them to commit murder? Wilson certainly could not have killed Sarah Ellis himself: too middle-aged, too flabby, too *detached* to sully his hands personally with such an activity. Livingstone was another matter. The back streets of Byker had spawned him; the river lands had been his track. He had fought his way out of the area to become a businessman in the shadow of Wilson but he still had the hands and the madness in his eyes to do the thing, if it was important enough to him. And money was important to him.

But could Albert Minford have any knowledge or understanding of all this? Arnold was half convinced that Minford had a corrupt streak. He had the gut feeling that the Amble project, and others, would have been the subject of subtle, indirect pressures from Councillor Minford, the kind that were not easily detectable but could result in favoured contracts for certain people. Blinds were drawn by declarations of interest, seemingly cleaning the activity. Behind the blinds more direct involvements could have occurred.

But it was still a far cry from murder.

Unhappily, Arnold paced around his room. He knew he would have an unsettled evening. He would not be able to concentrate, relax, for his mind would be filled with the churning possibilities that had been planted by the conversation with Ned Keeton.

He heard steps in the corridor, the murmur of voices. He hesitated, then walked across the room and opened the door. He saw the retreating forms of Wilson and Livingstone, the Senior Planning Officer leading them towards the lifts. The meeting was over. The fate of the inquiry into the Penbrook Farm scheme was probably sealed.

Arnold closed the door. He paced up and down, then went to the window. A corner of the car park was visible; there was a Ford Escort, two Vauxhalls, and the roof of a bigger car, a Rover, visible.

Someone was getting into the Rover, as he watched. He could not see the driver as the car nosed forward, disappeared from his view to the car park exit.

Edgily Arnold went back to his desk. He sat down, stared blankly at the papers there. On top of the papers was the crumpled message sheet the girl had given him, with the telephone message.

In a little while his eyes focused again. He read the number, and the message. It was from Ben Gibson. He had tried to ring Arnold; would Arnold be kind enough to ring him back?

Arnold would do better than that. He would go to see him.

* * *

The lights on the Tyne bridge were bright against the darkening sky and their reflection glinted and danced in the black waters of the river below. The Quayside was deserted at this early hour although the traffic that thundered over the bridge was still heavy, running south for the motorway.

It would, of course, have been easier for Arnold to have phoned the antiquarian, but he had been reluctant to go home to the bungalow, with the dark thoughts still churning in his head concerning the death of Sarah Ellis. He had decided on the spur of the moment to make the journey south to Newcastle. A discussion with Ben Gibson would take his mind off the murder at Penbrook Farm, he would be able to enjoy the company of the amiable eccentric for a little while, and then he would be able to walk up Dog Leap Stairs to Grey Street and indulge himself a little by having a quiet meal in the Italian restaurant he had frequented occasionally on his visits to Newcastle.

But first he enjoyed the stroll along the darkening waterfront. There were two freighters docked there: the timber loaded on the deck of the Norwegian vessel left a fresh smell in the evening air that reminded Arnold of his childhood: damp wood on summer evenings. The second vessel was bustling, preparing for a late evening tide that would take her down the winding river to the mouth of the Tyne and out to sea. Arnold thought he would like to be on her, sailing away from the niggling anxieties in his mind. For it was not only the thoughts of the possible guilts of Albert Minford and his acquaintances that were on his mind: oddly, Mildred Sauvage-Brown also bothered him.

He resented her presence in his thoughts. He had fixed her personality, determined what moved her, decided the kind of woman she was, some time ago, on the occasion of their early meetings. The image that had been presented at his bungalow had damaged that view. Her vulnerability, albeit a fleeting one, had disturbed him, cracked the edifice of personality he had constructed for her. And her loneliness had come too close to his own occasional feelings to be ignored. He had not suffered the loss she had, for Arnold had always been a solitary man; nevertheless, he was aware that the ache she felt was not one unfamiliar to himself. He had known empty, yawning evenings and the quiet darkness that seemed endless.

But her emotions were matters she could struggle with and overcome herself: she was strong enough to cope. He wanted no part of it all, so was annoyed that she still crept into his mind, an image, a dumpy, unattractive woman with a barbed tongue and an aggressive personality. The Quayside, he hoped, would dispel that image. Instead, strangely, it enhanced it.

He decided to go to Ben Gibson's house.

There were no lights in the upper floor windows: business, clearly, did not demand a burning of late electricity to fulfil small orders. Arnold rang the bell at the top of the stone stairs and then descended the short flight to stand in the doorway as a light flicked on behind the door. The steps shuffled along; the door opened and Ben Gibson stood hunched in the doorway, carrying a shotgun over his arm and peering suspiciously out at Arnold.

'It's me. Arnold Landon.'

Gibson coughed deep in his throat, an embarrassed sound, and lowered the muzzle. There was an expression of confusion on his ugly, squat features and he bobbed his head in apology. 'I'm sorry, Mr Landon. You should've said you were calling to see me. We get trouble around here from time to time. I can usually tell when; there's motorbikes tearing up and down the waterfront. But you can never be certain.'

He backed away, his arthritic bones making him shuffle like a crab. Arnold followed him into the passageway. 'That's the second time I've had a shotgun pointed at me in my life, and the first time was only a couple of weeks ago.'

'Oh?'

The tone did not imply Ben Gibson wanted to hear any more about shotguns; his embarrassment was such he wanted the incident forgotten. 'There's no shells in the gun,' he explained. 'It's just to frighten them away. They're only kids, really. And I'm an old man.'

It was as though he meant injuring an old man would be a matter of little consequence to the world. Perhaps, Arnold thought, he was right.

Ben Gibson broke the shotgun and set it down in a corner of the room where it was easily accessible. Clearly it wasn't the first time he had had occasion to take it up. He motioned Arnold to a chair and said, 'Visits in the early evening are unusual for me. I find them a little disturbing. It requires a little Armagnac to steady my nerves thereafter. Would you care to join me?'

'I'm sorry I disturbed you. I should have returned your call. However, a little sherry if you have any . . . ?'

The gnarled little man poured himself a drink and then opened a bottle of dark-coloured sherry. It was sweet and rich in taste. Arnold liked it. Ben Gibson's frog eyes observed him gently above his glass. He smiled. 'I'm pleased you called, Mr Landon, in spite of my nervousness. Your visits are few, but always welcome.'

Arnold was slightly embarrassed at the compliment. He nodded, smiled, and said, 'I got your message at the office, but thought it was time I took another trip to Newcastle. I presume your call concerned the sheet I left you?'

Ben Gibson nodded. He turned, walked across to the handsome mahogany bureau that stood against the far wall and fumbled for a key in the pocket of his faded waistcoat. He unlocked the bureau and from one of the pigeonholes extracted the sheet which Arnold had given him. He stared at it for several seconds with his back to Arnold: when he turned around Arnold could detect a certain sadness in the old man's face.

'It's been a pleasure to handle this sheet,' Ben Gibson said.

Arnold looked at him in surprise. 'It's valuable?'

Ben Gibson lifted a shoulder in a gesture of doubt. 'What is meant by the word? The sheet I hold here is rare. Its rarity makes it valuable. But do you measure value in currency of the realm? I think not. True values are held in the heart and in the mind, but especially in the heart.'

Arnold knew what he meant. He felt the same way. He had seen things in decayed villages that were treasures to him but were intrinsically of little value. 'What is the sheet, Mr Gibson?'

The old man did not answer him immediately. He sat down, handling the sheet with care, still gazing at it lovingly. Then he lifted his glass, sipped slowly at the Armagnac, and asked, 'You still cannot recall where you came upon this sheet?'

'No.'

'You know nothing of its provenance?'

'I'm afraid not.'

'A pity. A great pity.'

'Why?'

'It is very old.'

'And rare, you said.'

Ben Gibson nodded slowly. 'That is so. You see, the history of printing in England is such that by the end of the seventeenth century there were perhaps one hundred thousand titles printed. In the next hundred years that number leaped to some four hundred thousand: in other words, after 1695 there was an immense explosion of printing.'

'Why was that?'

'It was the result of the repeal of the Licensing Act.' Ben Gibson sipped his Armagnac. 'Under the Licensing Act, books could be printed only by members of the Stationers' Company. Members of the company had enjoyed that monopoly since 1555. The printing of books was in fact restricted to London, Oxford, Cambridge and York. But once the act was repealed the monopoly was destroyed and printing became possible in cities other than those towns.'

'And what does that mean as far as this sheet is concerned?' Arnold asked.

Ben Gibson frowned. 'I can't be sure, not precisely, but I can make an educated guess. Let's be clear about one thing. This sheet was not printed before 1695, but it's old. And rare. And there's a clue buried in it that interests me.'

'Clue?'

'It was perhaps natural that once the monopoly was removed from the Stationers' Company, other cathedral cities should establish their own presses. After all, printing was largely confined to the production of religious materials. One of the earliest attempts to found a new press was in the cathedral city of Durham. They used foreign know-how, naturally enough. A man called Gyseght, I believe. A Belgian. He established a press in Durham, under the auspices of the cathedral itself: they were enlightened enough in Durham not to believe the press to be the invention of the devil.'

'You think there's a connection between this sheet and the Durham cathedral press?'

Ben Gibson nodded. 'The press was established round about 1696. Gyseght was a vain man, proud of his skills and insistent on leaving his mark on all he printed. Accordingly, he marked the lower case g in the materials he printed, so that the work could be recognized as emanating from him, and his press.'

'It appears on this sheet?'

'I think it does,' Ben Gibson said gravely. 'Look.' He pointed to the crooked *g* in the third line of the Latin. 'I've inspected it closely with a magnifying glass. I'm pretty sure — sure as my old eyes can make me — that this sheet comes from a work printed by Gyseght in Durham.'

'When?' Arnold asked, a feeling of tight excitement rising in his chest.

'Ah, well, there you are,' Gibson replied. 'Fact is, the span of years during which Gyseght worked and the press flourished was narrow. The establishment at Durham was not a success. We can't be certain why, but the likelihood is Gyseght died without properly training a successor. Whatever happened, within eight years of its foundation the Durham press foundered. It was followed later, of course, by other presses, but the original establishment, the Gyseght foundation, lasted for just eight years.'

'And so, if this sheet comes from a book printed by Gyseght—'

'Its rarity value is high,' Gibson announced gravely. 'You must consider. A press founded after the repeal of the Licensing Act. One of only a few. It ended after only eight years — turn of the century. Its output would not have been great; the number of volumes that would have remained for twentieth-century eyes to see would inevitably have been few and located in the great museums: the British Museum, the Bodleian . . .'

'And this sheet—'

'Extremely rare.'

'And valuable.'

Ben Gibson was silent for a moment. Then he nodded, leaned forward and handed the sheet to Arnold. He looked sad.

'I told you,' Arnold said after a short silence, 'that you could keep it if you wished. I was only curious about it. For you—'

'Things would be different. I know,' Gibson said, his eyes large and luminous as he gazed at Arnold. 'I have made the study of such materials my life's blood. But a rarity of this kind . . . I would love to accept such an offer, if only of the single sheet. But — there is more.'

Arnold looked up from the sheet. 'What do you mean?'

'You still cannot recall where it was you found this sheet? How it came into your possession?'

Arnold shook his head. 'I'm at a loss. I've looked through all the books in my bungalow. I just can't recall . . .'

'It's important that you do recall. Try hard . . .'

* * *

The spaghetti carbonara was delicious. Arnold ordered a bottle of Valpolicella to wash it down, and then treated himself to a rare steak. He took no vegetables because the spaghetti had been filling, but as he toyed with the steak his mind was not really on the meal. He was still puzzled about the provenance of the sheet he had discussed with Ben Gibson.

The old man had refused Arnold's invitation to join him at the restaurant in Grey Street and Arnold had not been displeased for he wanted to think over the past days, consider deeply where he possibly could have found the sheet.

'It's clearly from a religious work,' Gibson had explained, 'a psalter, or a missal. And I have to tell you, the sheet itself is valuable. It would certainly bring you in a large sum from an enthusiastic collector. I can't name a figure: much depends upon whether there was an American bid. They rather . . . overvalue history sometimes. But if you could lay your hands on the whole book . . . if you had it on your shelves just waiting for this sheet to be returned to it, then we are talking not merely of a large sum of money, we are talking of a fortune . . .'

The trouble was, Arnold could not remember that there was anything on his shelves that remotely resembled an old missal. The books he had patiently sifted through in his sitting-room had been wide-ranging, but most were his own collection of materials that reflected his own passions: wood, stone, ancient buildings. There were old prints there, books of some rarity, but this sheet was something else again — a puzzle.

A puzzle to add to the other Ben Gibson had presented to him.

'It's important that you do recall. For there's more. It may well be that in your own interests you find few to talk to — an interest in old buildings among amateurs usually tends to be restricted to archways and configurations, local stone and steeples. I imagine your detailed knowledge and understanding is rare . . . It's not quite the same in my world. Antiquarian books . . . it's a passion that is shared by many, on a worldwide basis. And, inevitably, there is a network, a web of contacts that extends throughout this country and others. One has connections . . . we never meet, but information travels along the lines of communications like whispers over a telephone.'

'What sort of information?' Arnold had asked.

'Provenance, sometimes. More rarely, a ripple of excitement, a whisper that something unusual is coming on the market. And this is what has happened, literally within the last forty-eight hours. It has been whispered that a Gyseght book has been found and is to be auctioned.' The old man had paused dramatically. 'A Gyseght book . . . not perfect, but a find of huge value.'

'And you think—'

'Who can tell? Coincidence is the mainstay of existence. Whose life or career is truly planned? All I can say is two things: a Gyseght book is on the market at the time you find in your own home a sheet printed by the same man. Secondly, the whisper that a Gyseght is for sale was a whisper that was suddenly snuffed out.'

'You mean the work was withdrawn, or sold?'

'Those are two possibilities.'

'There is another?' Arnold had asked, half-guessing.

'There is.'

But it did not solve the puzzle that niggled away in Arnold's mind. He simply could not identify any of his books that might have a connection with the missal sheet, and he could not recall ever having seen the sheet, as a bookmark in any of his books, or in his house at all.

He had never seen it in his home. Arnold frowned, ordered a cappuccino and observed his image in the window of the restaurant. Tall, hunched, lean, his prominent nose shadowed by the overhead light . . . what had he actually done that particular day, the day he had found the sheet?

There had been his overcoat to repair: he had taken it to the cleaners. It had been crumpled on the back seat of his car since he had thrown it there after the arrest of Mildred Sauvage-Brown at Penbrook Farm.

Then there had been the compulsive need to clean the car inside and out. He had taken it to the car wash, aware of the impending return of the Senior Planning Officer.

And that had led him to the spring cleaning of his bungalow: gathering together the accumulation of newspapers and other clutter, emptying wastepaper baskets, throwing the lot in the dustbin and then . . . finding the sheet.

He shook his head. The coffee arrived. He stirred the chocolate gently into the coffee, still frowning. Dark streaks appeared in the creamy froth, uncertain, muddied as his mind. Muddied as Mildred Sauvage-Brown's campaign strategy. Mildred Sauvage-Brown . . .

He had never thought his mind could tingle. The feeling was one which he would have expected possible, physiologically, only at his nerve ends, under the skin. But he felt his mind tingle, was aware of something happening in his head, a dancing image that was just out of reach and yet sufficiently frightening to raise the short hairs on the back of his head.

Mildred Sauvage-Brown . . .

Mildred Sauvage-Brown at the inquiry before Mr Lansbury; tearing at his shoulder in the corridor; swinging her shotgun in a vain attempt to repel the police at Penbrook Farm. Images, pictures tumbling over and over in his brain . . . he closed his eyes tightly, until spots floated against a black background and when he opened them again the image reflected in the window shimmered and danced.

But Arnold hardly saw the mirror image; instead, he saw something else, a photograph, a group. He groaned. He thought of the photograph, and he thought of the events and the incidents and as the Italian waiter hovered with the bill he fitted them together, the photograph, the pictures in his mind, the tumbling events of the last few weeks.

And he worked out in his mind the provenance of the sheet from the Gyseght missal. More important perhaps, he worked out the implications of it all upon recent events.

CHAPTER FIVE

1

Arnold found the next two days agonizing.

The Senior Planning Officer had taken back the conduct of the Penbrook Farm application and Arnold was more than a little disturbed to learn that an approach had been made to the Chairman of the planning committee, Mr Lansbury, to have matters expedited. Arnold considered it dangerous: it would seem that the Senior Planning Officer was bowing to the pressures of big business and there were almost certainly going to be further whispers of local government chicanery current around Morpeth.

Surprisingly, there was no reaction from Mildred Sauvage-Brown. Arnold had expected she would come tearing into his office, or the Senior Planning Officer's, with loud and vociferous complaints about Lansbury's decision. Perhaps the death of Sarah Ellis had affected her deeply, so deeply that she had temporarily lost course, become unable to direct her thoughts positively towards the saving of Penbrook Farm. Or maybe she was, literally, defeated, her loneliness and loss destroying all sense of purpose.

There was nothing Arnold could do about it. He was no longer involved in the Penbrook Farm issues, and he had his own work to get on with. There were three new applications to process and the Willington Hall matter finally to set to rest. He phoned Henry Willington to tell him the sawmill development was now formally withdrawn and was not surprised at the reserved manner with which the heir to Willington received the news. Henry would have more on his plate than he had perhaps bargained for, with the estates inevitably having to be parcelled out for sale, merely to keep the house itself going.

But what really distressed Arnold was his inability to contact Freddie Keeler.

He had tried to reach him several times by phone. At first the girl in the office had been noncommittal: Mr Keeler was not available. Later, after the third call, she had reluctantly got through to the Warkworth office to make her own inquiries. She had called back to say that Mr Keeler was away on business.

Late the following afternoon Arnold called at Keeler's Newcastle office personally. The girl was darkly attractive but disinclined to be helpful. She was in no position to let Arnold have details of Mr Keeler's movements. Was he a tax inspector or something? Mr Keeler was certainly away on business, and it involved the sale of certain properties in Cleveland, *that* much she could divulge, but beyond that business ethics would not allow her to go, and Mr Landon shouldn't ask. 'I mean, if you're really a planning officer I might be giving away confidential information that would be damaging to Mr Keeler's business, mightn't I?'

So Arnold was left with the churning in his mind, the fear in his chest, and the gnawing anxiety that he should perhaps go to the police. But with what? Half baked theories, a sheet of paper that a Quayside eccentric said was valuable, and a conglomeration of wild accusations from a woman who had already spent a night in jail because of the violence of her behaviour.

That, and a Rover leaving the car park of the planning office at Morpeth.

It was hardly enough to bring anything but a rebuff from the police, and Arnold had already had a few of those in the last two years. So he kept his counsel and worried about the whereabouts of Freddie Keeler.

'Guisborough, man!' When Arnold finally reached the estate agent by phone the next morning there was exultation in the man's voice. 'I been staying in Guisborough, and I got a sweet deal all set up! There's a country house up there on the Cleveland Hills with about eighteen acres of prime land. The possibilities are ginormous—'

'Freddie, I need to see you.'

'Aye, man, so I gather, with all these phone calls and the pestering you been giving the girl here in the office. But I had to stay incognito, like, down in Guisborough because there's more than a few sharks prowling around, and I had this deal all set up and there was no way—'

'Freddie, where can we meet? It's *urgent*!'

They decided on the Duke of Wellington.

It was a convenient enough meeting place. It meant that Arnold could get there easily in his lunch break from the office, driving south along the winding country roads that snaked their way towards the sea, while Keeler could sensibly undertake the journey en route to his Warkworth office, which he had apparently neglected for some ten days.

The pub itself was on a rise, commanding views across the countryside and the sea; somewhat isolated for daily traffic, it nevertheless had a good catering reputation in the evenings and tended to draw numerous clients from the Alnwick and Morpeth areas. Today, the car park was almost empty and the lounge bar was quiet. Arnold sat there with a glass of lager in front of him and waited for Freddie Keeler to arrive.

He was fifteen minutes late when he breezed in, ordered himself a gin and tonic and swaggered across to join Arnold. 'Hey, what a day, man! Finally got rid of two houses up on the Town Moor, and clinched the Guisborough deal as well as shifting a couple off arms up Rothbury way. I tell you, life's looking good at the moment.'

He shrugged himself out of his trench coat and sat down, looking pleased with himself. 'Now then, laddie, what's the trouble? How can Uncle Freddie help?'

Now that he was face to face with the estate agent, Arnold found it difficult to explain. 'I . . . I want some information,' he began lamely.

Keeler looked at him with a cautious air. 'Now hold on, bonny lad. You're a planning officer; I'm an estate agent. There's not going to be any sort of *confidential* stuff you want to prise out of me, is there? About my mates in the business, that sort of thing?'

'It's got nothing to do with your business . . . not the house purchase side, at least.'

Keeler looked puzzled. He sipped his gin and tonic. 'Well, let's have it out, lad. I'm not a mind-reader. What is it you want from me, hey?'

'We talked, recently,' Arnold began cautiously.

'Aye.'

'About the auction rings.'

Keeler frowned, and stared for a few moments at his gin. 'I recall. But that's . . . well . . .'

'There's no threat in this, Freddie,' Arnold hastened to say.

'That's as may be. But the auctions, well, they're a bit delicate, you know, Arnold? I wouldn't want you to be asking around about them too much. I mean, I said a bit more than I should have, and there are some heavy lads among the interested parties, you know? They're not above lifting the odd boot if they feel they've been shopped.'

'Believe me—'

'All right, just so long as you know the score,' Keeler said heavily. 'What do you want to know?'

'I want to know whether there's an auction ring arranged soon.'

Keeler frowned. 'A ring? You mean, is there anything planned for a knock-out agreement?' He shook his head. 'Not to my knowledge, Arnold. I mean, there's been no decent sale on for the last month or so. There's one planned in about six weeks that'll bring in the sharks. Furniture mainly, but there's a couple of pieces that the lads will be working on, I reckon.'

Arnold hesitated. 'I'm not thinking so much of a knock-out agreement operating after a sale. I want to know whether there's likely to be a private auction occurring, just with dealers involved and no publicity.'

Freddie Keeler stared at him for several seconds, then slowly shook his head. 'I think you got things wrong, Arnold. A *private* deal? No, things don't work like that in the rings. A private deal of the kind I think you're talking about comes about only when there's specialist stuff on the market, and when its provenance is . . . shall we say, a bit doubtful? Then, the word goes out on the grapevine, and the dealers gather. They're a bit like vultures, I tell you,' he added feelingly, 'and the whole thing's a bit too rich for *my* blood. I mean, there's *real* money flowing around on those occasions.'

'Are you in touch with that kind of grapevine?' Arnold asked.

Freddie Keeler finished his drink, rose and walked to the bar. He ordered another drink for himself and one for Arnold, but there was a slightly truculent air about him as he sat down again. 'Look, I told you this was a specialized sort of operation. The links are different — depending on what the items are. And, well, outsiders ain't exactly welcome. Arrivals at the rings, they're by invitation only, you know what I mean? So you got to be careful. Me, I can't say any more unless I know what it's all about.'

Arnold hesitated. 'What do you need to know?'

Keeler leaned forward conspiratorially. 'First of all, the nature of the items.'

'There's only one.'

'*One*?' Keeler's eyes widened. 'So what is it?'

'A book.'

Keeler was about to snort in derision but the noise died. He sat back, eyeing Arnold carefully. 'One item. A book. It's got to be bloody old, then.'

'That's right.'

Keeler screwed up his features in thought and contemplated the ceiling. 'Yeah, all right, I got a few connections I could sound out, but I'm not certain they'll come through. Not unless I had a good story.'

'What kind of story?'

'To explain your interest.'

Again Arnold hesitated. He was not certain how much to tell Freddie Keeler; uncertain how much he had yet even substantiated in his own mind. He shook his head reluctantly. 'It's a delicate matter, Freddie.'

'Most business deals are.'

'Business?'

'Oh, come on, Arnold. You're not really interested in books. Not unless they're about bloody stone or wood. And I have a gut feeling, from the way you've been sweating after me that this isn't interest, it's business!'

'Well . . .'

'I'm the soul of discretion,' Keeler said, 'and I love the idea of you coming down from your bloody pedestal to dirty your hands in the commercial market.'

'The book is an old one, Freddie.'

'So you tell me.'

'It's worth a great deal of money.'

'A *great* deal?'

'That's right.'

Freddie Keeler's eyes shone wetly. 'And where do you come in, Arnold?'

'The book . . . it's an old missal, or psalter, printed in Durham at the end of the seventeenth century. It's worth a lot of money, even though it's not perfect.'

'*Perfect?*'

'It's been damaged. Pages missing. Maybe only one page.'

'And?'

'I can lay my hands on that page, I think.'

Freddie Keeler whistled, then smiled broadly. 'You cunning old bugger! I always had you marked for the character who'd hand over any find to what they call the proper authorities! But you're not above making a few bob yourself, then! What's the pitch?'

'The sheet came into my possession,' Arnold said. 'I need not explain how.'

'Mum's the word, boy,' Keeler cackled delightedly.

'I discovered what it was, but was told that the book itself was being made available for sale . . . Almost immediately, the sale went underground.'

'That's the pattern, boy, that's the pattern. They'll have valued the thing, realized questions might be asked, the bloody heritage merchants will be sniffing around, so they'll go to private auction, invite them with rich blood, and the book will quietly disappear into some collection and a lot of money will change hands. With no export licences being called for!'

Arnold was still vague about what best to tell the estate agent, but the line he was pursuing seemed fruitful so he plunged on. 'What you have to realize, Freddie, is that while the book is extremely valuable — even imperfect — its value will increase significantly if it were a perfect copy.'

'I'm ahead of you, bonny lad, I'm streets ahead of you. There's no way you'd be in the market for buying a book like that, but you're in the market for *selling*!' Keeler chortled happily. 'What a turn-up! A single bloody sheet and you can make a bomb, just playing the buggers off against each other, and you end up with a tidy sum and no risks while they pay you through the nose in order to heighten their own profit margins. Arnold, you're on a winner!'

'If I can reach the auction,' Arnold reminded him.

Keeler frowned darkly, his excitement evaporating. 'Aye, point taken. Well, look, old son, tell you what I'll do. I said I had a few contacts. I'll try them; have to be discreet, of course, and if I come up with anything . . . well, it'll be up to you. Dicey business getting you into the ring. They'd be too suspicious. And I got my own reputation to consider. Don't want to be seen as unreliable, like. But if I do get the word, it's yours. And my best advice would be to find out who the buyer is, then approach him. Won't get the best deal that way — playing them all might be better, because they're greedy sods, but it's safer. Suss out who's the buyer.'

'It was something like that,' Arnold admitted, 'I was considering.'

'Arnold, my friend, leave it to me. So drink up: there's time for another!'

2

Arnold always felt that the further north he drove, the greater became the raw flavour of frontier country. It seemed to hang in the wind as he drove along the looping road, rising over the fells with the Cheviot menacing to his left and distant sea views to his right. He dipped down to cross winding streams and rose to pass craggy outcrops of rock where sixteenth-century Scottish pirates had camped, while the distinctive sea tang drifted in from the shores beyond Bamburgh and the hoary old sea-castle built by King Ida the Flamebearer.

'Lindisfarne,' Freddie Keeler had said to him over the phone. 'For God's sake don't ask me why. All I can suggest is that the guy who's selling the book wants the transaction in as out of the way place as possible. All right, it's common practice for the auction rings to go to some quiet place, well away from snoopers and possible police activity, but this character must be really shy if he's chosen Lindisfarne! But you nail 'em, Arnold. Nail 'em for every penny they got!'

He had taken a day's leave from work. The Senior Planning Officer had raised no objection: Arnold had some leave due to him. Moreover, he had kept a low profile during the days since the Senior Planning Officer's return, and perhaps had given the impression he had been chastened by the tongue-lashing he had received.

Had the Senior Planning Officer been aware of Arnold's intentions he would have been apoplectic.

Arnold was not sure of his intentions himself. He had not been entirely honest with Freddie Keeler, of course: he had no intention of selling the sheet from the missal, or of trying to set bidders at each other's throats. Nor was he particularly interested in who was going to buy the book; rather, he was interested in the name of the person selling it. The thought itself caused a cold prickle at the back of his neck. He was half-hoping he was making a bad mistake over the missal, but he had to find out. If his suspicions were justified, on the other hand, he was not sure what he would do. *One step at a time*, he muttered to himself, *one step at a time.*

He had planned his day carefully. He rose at nine and made himself a good breakfast, to quell the nervousness in his stomach as much as anything else. Then he chose warm clothing, for he had the feeling he might be in for a long, cold wait.

He set off at ten-thirty, armed with two flasks of hot coffee, safely stowed in the back of the car. He had dawdled into Warkworth and had a light lunch at The George, then taken the A1 north again, past the scattered pele towers on the road to Bamburgh.

It was early afternoon when the country had opened out and the signs beckoned him to Berwick; he turned off, took the road beyond Dunstanburgh Castle and travelled parallel to the main road — a longer route, but one he felt safer on in his nervous state.

The narrow roads twisted their way northwards and he thought about the old Lindisfarne, the austerity of which must have suited Aidan and his band of Irish monks who had settled there in the seventh century to establish the Celtic church and evangelize the North. Things were different now: the abbey had been destroyed centuries ago and remained only as a gaunt, ribbed tourist attraction, the castle had a fairy-tale appearance crowning the rock above the island in its Lutyens restoration and under the care of the National Trust, and it was bric-a-brac and Lindisfarne Mead, a rugged coastline and the feeling of isolation from the mainland, that brought the tourist throngs in the summer.

But for Arnold, some things would never change. Only sixty miles from Newcastle, Lindisfarne, the Holy Island, nevertheless had retained its remoteness, closed off as it was for three hours either side of each high tide. Arnold drove across the narrow causeway in the late afternoon as a pale sun glistened on the sinisterly named sands — the Swad, and the Slakes — and the stone causeway was still wet and smelling of the sea as the dark water lapped at its edge. He could imagine it as little different from the days when the Danes had marauded ashore to burn the abbey, and the day in 875 when the monks, fearful for their precious relics, had finally departed to the south and Durham, with their priceless Lindisfarne Gospels.

Arnold shivered, and carefully drove his car off the causeway into the sheltering dunes, piled high by the wind from the Fame Islands. He turned off his engine and the silence drifted in upon him. He would have to wait now, he guessed, until the Fame lights were blinking in the dusk above the sea.

He had no plan of action as such. The word from Freddie Keeler had been that the meeting was to be held at Lindisfarne at a pub, The Dog and Whistle. He could not tell Arnold of the scheduled time: his informant had given him basic information but had Freddie pressed for more detail suspicion would have crept in. Nor could Freddie discover who had been invited to the auction, but it was not due to start until about eight in the evening.

Arnold had decided to arrive early for one simple reason: he wanted to have a view of who might be driving across the causeway to the auction.

From his parking spot he could see a stretch of some fifty yards of the causeway, while the shoulder of the dune hid his own car from the drivers on the road: they would be sweeping past before they could see him and it was unlikely they would even notice him. And if they did, he would probably be dismissed as a birdwatcher, or a courting couple. He waited, opened his first flask, found the coffee hot and watched the glistening Slake as a cold wind came in from the sea to carry the unearthly crooning of eider ducks, floating on the dark sea below the grassy cliffs of the distant Heugh.

Two cars drove across the causeway but they were of little interest to Arnold: small and battered, they probably belonged to local families, gone for the day to Berwick, perhaps. The men Arnold expected would come in bigger vehicles than these.

He considered again the warning words Freddie Keeler had uttered on the phone. 'And let's get one thing straight, Arnold — I don't know anything about all this. I don't want to know. Things can get rough with some of these merchants — they're not exactly Debrett.'

'I'll remember that,' Arnold had assured him.

'And one more thing, my son. Keep your eyes peeled, because you're not alone, kiddar.'

'How do you mean?'

'I told you. I had to tread careful when I was asking around. All right, I got the information in the end but it wasn't easy, especially since I wasn't the only one asking questions.'

'I don't understand.'

'Neither do I. But I'm telling you. You haven't been the first asking questions about the auction.'

'You mean a possible bidder?'

'No. Not so. I told you: auctions like this are by invitation only. You don't ask your way in. I been asking around to find out where and when; it seems someone else has been doing the same thing. And that makes people edgy. What about your own informant?'

'Informant?'

'The guy who identified the sheet for you.'

Ben Gibson. 'No, I hardly think he'd make inquiries.'

'Well, I'm telling you facts, old son. So go canny.'

Arnold waited. Dusk was falling and the lights were twinkling on in the scattered houses on the island. A gash of red glinted across the sky, outlining the castle on its rock, towering gauntly over the village, and high in the night sky an intermittent flashing heralded a jet plane flying north.

Seabirds and seals, wild geese, dunes, deep shining sands. An unearthly place, and the coughing roar of a vehicle approaching at speed across the causeway. Arnold wound down his window in the gathering dusk and peered out, smelling the sea tang and feeling the cold wind bite at his cheek.

It was a Land Rover. Driven at speed, probably a local again, hurrying home before dark. Arnold checked his watch: it was near seven. Soon, he guessed, they would come.

They did, at last, some forty minutes later, not in convoy but at short intervals. Deep-throated cars, big cars, bright headlights lancing along the Slake and past the dunes towards the quiet village.

Arnold counted them.

Eight, before the silence swept in from the sea again, and it was time he himself moved.

Arnold started his car and drove carefully out of the dunes towards the lights of the village.

* * *

He parked at the top end of the village, near the area reserved for tourists queuing for their ration of free Lindisfarne Mead before they bought a bottle. The streets near the tiny village square were quiet enough, curtains drawn at the windows, and Arnold walked slowly down the main road, past the Land Rover parked awkwardly, half on the pavement, until he came to the top of the hill.

The evening was not dark; a crescent moon silvered the sea beyond Lindisfarne Castle, where the black ribs of the old staithes jutted out starkly against the twisting ripples. The abbey stood to his right, its ruined walls lurching against the sky, but just below the abbey, where the lane started, twisting down towards the shoreline, several cars were parked.

Arnold hesitated. It would be impossible for him to gain entry to the auction, and he did not know the man — or woman — he was looking for. The cars — big and powerful — would be owned by the men he sought, but when they finally left how was he to distinguish one from another?

Thoughtfully he walked down towards the cars. As he drew near he saw that among them was a Porsche and two Rovers: the moneymen were here. He looked about him, gazed towards the abbey and the small burial ground on the hill and then he walked back to his car. When he returned to the abbey lane he was carrying his binoculars.

He would see little in the evening light, but the lens of the binoculars might help. Carefully he made his way up to the cemetery on the hill, his feet crunching lightly on the sandy track, until he reached a vantage-point near the abbey walls. He stood uncertainly for a while, and then found a convenient gravestone against which to lean. He focused the binoculars and began a slow sweep of all the houses in the vicinity of the parked cars.

The cottages, their doors and windows, crept darkly into his view. There were occasional lights, a few lit windows, but nothing of interest. He reached the doors of the pub, the Dog and Whistle, and there was a scattering of cars in the narrow park, lights blazing in the bar and lounge, but the frosted windows gave him no insight. Then, almost as an afterthought, Arnold elevated the binoculars to the upstairs windows.

They had been careless.

Although the group had parked their cars in the lane, well away from the pub, and walked along the road, one by one, they had felt themselves secure in the private upstairs room of the Dog and Whistle and had drawn no curtains. The hill on which Arnold had positioned himself, however, gave him an advantage: with the aid of the binoculars he could see into the room.

Not that he could see a great deal. A few heads and shoulders, a certain movement as men walked about, talking to acquaintances, a general casual movement which suggested to Arnold they had not got down to serious business yet.

Then one familiar head came into view; Arnold struggled with the focusing, to sharpen the image, but he already knew who the man was. Freddie Keeler had told him previously that Wilson was interested in the auction rings, and now the evidence lay before Arnold. Wilson was at the upstairs gathering in the Dog and Whistle.

They seemed to be settling down as he watched, drawing up chairs, arranging themselves in a more formal fashion. One man sat with his back to the window, and again Arnold considered the set of the shoulders familiar but he could not be certain. And there was one man standing. He appeared to be speaking to the gathering. Desperately Arnold tried to make out who he was, guessing that the man would be the seller, the person putting up the missal for bids. In an attempt to get a better angle, away from the obstruction of the man near the window, Arnold moved, stepping away from his vantage-point. His shoes crunched on gravel; at the same moment he heard something away to his left.

Arnold stopped, gazed around carefully, but among the shadowed, leaning tombstones nothing moved and gradually the prickling feeling at the back of his neck subsided. Graveyards at night were not exactly the most soothing places to be, he considered. He took up a new position, near a stunted tree, and applied the binoculars again to the upstairs room of the Dog and Whistle.

The man was someone he had never seen before.

He was a thin, small man, bald, with glasses. He was dressed in a dark suit and he made much use of his hands. There was no doubt in Arnold's mind that the man was conducting the sale; equally, there was no doubt that he was a professional. His gestures, his movements told Arnold the man had done this before.

The seller was using an agent.

It meant further problems for Arnold. He could not be certain the seller was in the room at the Dog and Whistle now. He might be, and Arnold had counted on that event, but using an agent meant the seller might be in the room, incognito, or he might be elsewhere, awaiting the moment when the agent could report the sale completed.

The situation seemed to be slowing in the upstairs room. The little bald man was more hesitant, less frenetic in his gestures. They were nearing the market price. Even as Arnold realized it, the little bald man suddenly clapped his hands together, was smiling broadly and then bobbed his head as he reached forward to pick something up. It was a glass. He raised it and drank.

The sale had been completed.

Arnold lowered the binoculars. He leaned back against the weathered bark of the tree and the blood began to pound in his head. He was not sure that he should be here at all. He should have gone to the police. But with what? For that matter, what did he have now? Precious little. A face — a small, bald man with glasses. And a theory.

He waited.

He checked his watch in the faint light. The group would be forced to break up within the next ten minutes or so if they were to be absolutely certain of making it back to the mainland. From the information he had received, the tide would be on the turn and within half an hour the causeway at the Slakes would be awash, impassable for cars. It was always best to give the tide a good twenty minutes either side before its run, for when the water did cut off Lindisfarne from the mainland it came in at the speed of a racehorse.

Someone was leaving the Dog and Whistle. A tall man, he walked confidently and quickly, down towards the cars parked in the lane below the ruined abbey. Arnold focused on him as he drew near, passing the lighted window of one of the cottages below. The face was unfamiliar. The man entered the Porsche: in two minutes its rear lights were glowing on the hill as he braked at the bend. A moment later he was lost to sight and the thunder of his engine was a distant sound.

A second man left the inn. His head was lowered and he walked quickly, as though seeking to avoid recognition. Arnold could not make out his face and when he entered one of the Rovers Arnold became agitated, craning forward to try to make out the man's features.

When the Rover manoeuvred out of the lane Arnold was in a quandary. There had been a Rover in the car park at Morpeth; a Rover had been spotted the night Sarah Ellis had been battered to death. Anxiously Arnold watched as the car accelerated away up the hill, then he swung his binoculars back to the upstairs room in the Dog and Whistle. He drew in his breath sharply: the man whose head and shoulders he had thought familiar was now standing, stretching lithely. It was Livingstone.

And even as he watched, Wilson came back into the line of sight. It was not he who had left in the Rover. Both Wilson and Livingstone had been present at the auction; both were still there, and there was still one Rover left parked in the lane.

Arnold waited, glancing anxiously at his watch. They would be cutting things fine. Unless they had decided to stay for the night on the island. Even as he thought so, he realized the party in the upstairs room was breaking up. Another two men emerged from the inn and started to walk down towards the lane. Arnold bobbed about, trying to get a better line of sight and away to his left he heard a rushing, rustling noise, as though he had disturbed something, a sheep perhaps, or a nocturnal animal. He focused on the small group, but could not make out whether Wilson or Livingstone were included. Car doors were being banged, as two more men came down the hill, headlights flashed on and car engines coughed into life.

Arnold realized he was in an impossible situation. He could not sensibly see who was leaving; he had no idea which of these men the auctioneer would have been working for;

and even if he could identify him, unless he actually *recognized* him he would be unable to give effectual chase because his own car lay in the park at the top end of the village.

He started to hurry forward, through the graveyard, dodging his way through a scattering of leaning headstones until he reached the grassy knoll above the lane. He slowed, cautiously, and checked the cars. The second Rover had left the lane in the interval while he had been scrambling forward.

But the little man with the bald head was walking past the lane, down towards the gate leading to Lindisfarne Castle.

Arnold hesitated. The man was walking purposefully, his bald head glistening in the faint light of the crescent moon, and he had his head down, scuttling along as though he were in a hurry. He was some twenty yards past Arnold before Arnold took the decision to follow him.

It was easy enough.

Beyond the lane the road ended. A rough track, worn and rutted from the cars that drove there in the summer months to park along the shoreline, led to the National Trust gateway which barred casual visitors. The gate was open now, and the auctioneer was hurrying through it, but Arnold made little sound as he followed him, keeping to the grass verge and moving swiftly.

Ahead of them loomed the turreted castle on its black, craggy rock.

Once the auctioneer had moved along the track to the right of the castle he would be climbing on rising ground. It was possible then for Arnold to throw aside caution and hurry around the left side of the crag, climb over the rocky base until he reached the bank that led down to the shoreline and come up behind the auctioneer and the person he was meeting.

As he hurried along Arnold recalled he had seen neither Wilson nor Livingstone go to the cars in the lane, and it would have been easy for either — or both of them — to leave the inn unseen from a side entrance and make it to the headland before the auctioneer arrived.

Arnold reached the foot of the crag and scrambled over the rough rocks, grabbing at the tussocky grass to pull himself up swiftly. He was in the shadow of the castle now and made no attempt to quieten his progress: the auctioneer would be unable to hear him from the other side of the crag.

Twenty yards above him the moonlight gleamed faintly on the rock and as he drew near the top of the bank Arnold moved more cautiously. To the left of the crag, and some thirty yards from the track that wound up along the side of the rock to the castle gateway there were three humped structures. They were the hulls of fishing boats, Arnold recalled, which had been turned over, had doorways fashioned in them, and were now used as storage huts. Arnold moved towards them carefully, and the faint sound of voices drifted to him on the night air.

He crouched, uncertain how far to proceed, and then the matter was resolved for him. A car engine coughed into life and headlights whitened the crag below the castle. The light swung, moved across the crag and lit up the track leading back towards the village. As the engine roared in the darkness Arnold stood upright, realizing he had made a bad miscalculation.

Wildly he scrambled up the last few yards of the bank, reached the side of the inverted hulls and burst past them to the path beyond. The little auctioneer had not heard his approach and as Arnold rushed out from behind the hulls he gave a startled yelp, raised his hands in alarm and then shot off like a startled rabbit towards the headland.

Arnold ignored him. He was interested only in the vehicle and it was already at the top of the track. All he could see of it was the rear lights, glowing as the vehicle dipped over the ridge. Angrily Arnold ran forward as the driver disappeared over the ridge.

When Arnold had followed the little auctioneer he had made a mistake. He had never considered that the man selling the missal might have arranged to meet the auctioneer privately, on the headland; and he had certainly not guessed that the man would have kept his car parked near the hulls below the castle. Arnold should have considered it, thought of it earlier, but it was too late now as he ran after the car, shouting desperately.

At the top of the ridge Arnold stopped for a moment, breathing hard as anger and frustration seized him. He was not thinking straight. In his excitement he had not considered the auctioneer. He should have grabbed the man, questioned him, forced from him the identity of the man who had instructed him in the sale of the missal. Arnold looked back but he could see only the rocky coastline and the darkness of the sky. The startled auctioneer had fled beyond the hulls and would already be halfway back to the safety of the village lights, a mile away. Either that, or he would be out there on the shoreline, hiding.

Arnold turned again, to glare after the receding lights of the car. He knew there was no chance of catching it now, but even as he told himself so he gained the impression that the vehicle was slowing below him on the track. Arnold hesitated, puzzled, and then he guessed what was happening.

On the rutted track progress would be difficult. Perhaps the driver had gone too quickly in his eagerness; wheelspin might have slowed him, even brought him to a halt on the broken, rutted ground. There might yet be the opportunity to catch up with him and excitement surged again in Arnold's chest. He began to run down from the ridge.

The sandy loam crunched under his feet and as he came down the slope he felt almost that he was flying. The track curved away below him, rounding the shoulder of the crag, and the vehicle ahead still seemed to be in difficulty, struggling across the bumpy ruts, its engine whining away in the night air. Arnold hurried down the slope and reached the bottom of the crag but then he too found the going far from easy. The ruts were difficult to make out in the darkness, the uneven surface was dangerous underfoot and he fell, twice, losing his rhythm and lurching along the rutted track, until he took the precaution of stepping aside to the grassy verge where he was able to pick up speed.

Ahead of him, the vehicle was nearing the gateway to the road. Arnold could smell exhaust fumes in the air and the engine was roaring desperately as the driver fought the wheel, bucking the car across the furrows, sliding it nearer the entrance. Arnold tried to increase his own speed but the breath was whistling in his chest and his lungs were aching at the unaccustomed exercise and excitement. He was still some thirty yards from the car when the engine roar became steadier, throaty, the rear lights swung wildly, then straightened, and the driver forced his vehicle through the gateway, colliding with the gate as he did so.

Arnold knew he was finished. He could never catch the car now. Furious with himself for his lack of foresight and for his incompetence, he watched helplessly as the vehicle gathered speed, headlights flickering up as it reached the lane at the bottom of the hill and wound its way past the abbey and up the hill.

Arnold slowed to a gentle trot. It was hopeless. He was reluctant to give up the chase and doggedly he kept going, but it was with a sense of angry despair. He lurched along the track to the gate and the lights of the car disappeared around the bend above, heading into the village. Arnold trotted past the lane, and the vantage-point he had held in the graveyard, but there were no cars parked at this end of the track now.

The Dog and Whistle was still ablaze with light and someone was singing in the bar, a broken version of the Keel Row, but Arnold staggered past the inn door, feeling the leadenness of his legs increase as he turned onto the hill to make his way past the stretch of cottages leading up to the main square.

At the top of the rise someone was starting a car. Its headlights glowed fiercely at him for a few moments, then the vehicle was reversed into a side street, to come out again in a charging rush, swinging wildly into the street. Arnold had his head down, gasping as he toiled up the hill. The blood was pounding in his head and there was a lancing pain in his chest. He slowed to a walk; to continue running was stupid. The chase was over.

His chest heaving, he walked quietly through the village towards the square, where he had left his car. When he reached it he stood there for several minutes, leaning against it, waiting for the pounding of his blood to subside and his breathing to return to normal. Then, painfully, he unlocked the car and climbed inside.

He felt completely dispirited. His journey to Lindisfarne had been wasted. He had discovered nothing beyond the fact that both Wilson and Livingstone had been at the auction. He had no idea who the auctioneer was, and he had no idea which of the two men had instructed him in the sale of the missal. Arnold had misjudged the whole situation, made a fool of himself, and run the risk of breaking his neck in the darkness of the rutted track.

Despondently he started the car.

His clothing was stained with mud and there was a damp patch on his knee where he had fallen in the wet, tussocky grass. He felt stupid, and as he drove along the lane out of the village, back towards the Slakes, he cast gloomily over the events of the last hour, hardly aware of the road ahead of him, contemplating miserably the incompetent manner in which he had conducted himself. Now, he could not imagine what on earth had possessed him, trying to discover for himself the man who had sold the missal. He was not suited to the role of detective: there were professionals who did this sort of thing, and did it far more efficiently.

There was a rushing sound under the wheels of the car, and Arnold blinked. For several seconds he was puzzled, as the noise increased and he felt the car slow, not responding properly to the accelerator. Then his eyes widened as he saw the black stretch of water in his headlights, and he realized how he had compounded all the foolishness of the last few hours in a dangerous fashion.

He had forgotten the tide and the causeway.

He took his foot off the accelerator in panic and braked; a moment later, he surged the car forward again. He had no idea what to do. The water was lifting in a bow spray in front of him, he could not see the road ahead and he knew that if he tried to turn he ran the risk of plunging off the road itself into the soft sand. There was no turning back, even though he was only a hundred yards or so along the causeway, and he knew he stood no chance of getting right across to the mainland. His hands were frozen to the steering-wheel and his mind spun in wild panic as he drove on, helplessly, until the car engine coughed and spluttered, sea water drenching the plugs and killing the ignition.

The car shuddered to a stop. Arnold stared helplessly out of the window. The water looked black now, spreading all about him, marooned on the causeway. Desperately he tried to calm himself, think what best to do. Chances were that as the tide came racing in it would lift the car, deposit it in the deeper water and he would be forced to climb . . .

Climb.

Of course. In his panic, he had forgotten. Marooned vehicles were not an uncommon experience on the causeway. Particularly during the summer months, tourists were constantly being trapped on the causeway, ignorant of the speed with which the tide came in, risking the trip back to the mainland even though they could see part of the causeway under water. Arnold should never have attempted the drive, would not have attempted it but for his gloomy introspection, but though he was trapped he recalled now that provision had been made for fools such as he. Half way across the causeway there was a refuge, a hut built on stilts to keep it well above the tidewater. In the summer it was a regular occurrence for helicopters to be called out to lift off stranded motorists. There would be no helicopter tonight, but the refuge was there.

If Arnold could reach it in time.

He got out of the car, stepping gingerly down to the roadway. The black water swirled around his legs, reaching almost to his knees and he felt the panic rise in his chest again, for he had no idea how far he might be from the refuge. The moonlight had faded and the sky darkened; he could make out dimly a stake driven into the sand at the side of the roadway and he knew that there would be a succession of these, marking out the causeway itself. He needed to move from one to the next, taking care not to step off the roadway into the treacherous sand of the Slakes.

He could feel the drag of the tide against his calves as he began to walk, quickly, thrusting through the water with a long stride. His movements caused the water to swirl higher against his knees and as he progressed from one stake to the next he realized that the tide was truly ripping in across the sands at speed. Moreover, the causeway dipped slightly as it reached the halfway point and the water would be deeper there. He had to hurry.

He hurried. The drag grew stronger against his legs and as he struggled from one stake to the next in line the splashing surge soaked his thighs. Two minutes later he was aware of the increased depth as the coldness seeped across his hips. He knew he could not be far from the refuge but he still could not see it in the dim light.

To make matters worse it began to rain, a light drifting wetness that rapidly soaked his hair and began to drip down his face. He could see no lights ahead of him on the mainland and none behind him from the village. He was aware of the distant sound of sea surge beyond the dunes, but closer at hand the lapping rush of the tide panicked him, as he seemed to be trapped in a dark, wet world where the coldness reached up towards his chest.

Walking was more difficult now. The tide was running in fast and the water was up to his waist so that he had to throw his arms wide to retain balance as he forced himself along the causeway. He tried to keep the fear in check; the refuge could not be far distant, but he still could see nothing and his heart was beginning to pound uncomfortably.

He had been a fool to ever attempt the crossing; he had been a bigger fool ever to come north to Holy Island.

Something dark loomed up in front of him and Arnold stopped.

For a moment he thought it was the refuge and then realized it could not be, for it was not high enough, or bulky enough. He peered ahead, waded a few more steps, and then realized that he was not the only person trapped on the causeway. He remembered now, when he was struggling up the hill, a vehicle had started up in the village, hurried out into the lane. The driver had been trying to beat the tide and now, like Arnold, was trapped. It was a relief to know there was more than one fool in the world, Arnold considered, and thrust his way forward towards the vehicle.

It was a Land Rover. He had expected it to be empty, but it was not. As he drew level with it, a window was wound down. Arnold looked up, peering incredulously at the face staring down at him.

'What on earth are you doing here?' he asked.

'I'm scared,' said Mildred Sauvage-Brown.

3

The rain had increased in intensity and the sky had darkened even further as Arnold persuaded Mildred Sauvage-Brown to step down from the vehicle. She tried to argue at first, complaining that she would be safe from the tide in the Land Rover, but Arnold insisted she come with him, for neither of them was certain how high the tide would rise, and they would be completely safe only in the refuge.

She came splashing down beside him and she clung to his arm in a manner distinctly unlike the usual Mildred. He felt her fingers biting into the muscle of his arm and she was shuddering, perhaps with the coldness of the water, but possibly out of sheer fear. Arnold half dragged her forward as the blackness surged coldly about them and her fear caused his own to ebb as he concentrated on pulling her along with him. It was clear in moments, however, that she had stalled the Land Rover only a matter of twenty yards from the refuge, for it loomed out of the darkness on its long stilts, only a short distance ahead of them.

Arnold raised his face against the rain. 'You should have gone straight to the refuge, instead of huddling there in the Land Rover.'

She shook her head, saying nothing, and the fingers were still fierce on his arm as he dragged her towards the ladder that reached up to the haven above.

She seemed unwilling to go up first, but Arnold insisted short-temperedly, pushing her to the rungs and shoving her from below when she seemed reluctant to step upwards. It was unreasonable, he felt, with the cold black water swirling around his hips, for her to argue silently in this manner against taking what was the obvious step, and reach for the safety of the refuge. 'Get on,' he shouted. 'Hurry up there before we catch our death of cold, let alone drown!'

She began to climb the ladder. Arnold grabbed at the rungs, began to lift himself out of the water, his head butting against her leg and he shouted at her again, in exasperation. 'There's nothing to be scared of! Get on! I tell you there's nothing to be scared of!'

But there was. Arnold realized it at once when the voice came to them from the darkness above.

'Come on,' the man said, 'I'll give you a hand.'

And Arnold knew why Mildred Sauvage-Brown had been scared.

* * *

The refuge was small and dark. It smelled of wet timber, and it was unfurnished, with no heating, but then, it was not intended as anything other than a temporary refuge.

'There is a phone,' the man said, 'to be used for emergency purposes. Bloody thing's broken, isn't it! Typical. Anyway, we're safe enough, as long as we don't succumb to pneumonia. You smoke?'

Neither Arnold nor Mildred Sauvage-Brown replied.

They were standing close together, huddled near the doorway, and the other occupant of the refuge was leaning against the wall, some six feet away. In the darkness it was impossible to make out his features, but Arnold could hear him fumbling in his pocket for cigarettes.

'Can't imagine how you two came to take the chance on the causeway. I just wasn't thinking. I had to get back to the mainland, and when I started on the causeway I thought I could still make it. But that damned tide comes in at a hell of a lick. I got past the refuge all right, maybe half a mile on but the car just died on me. I thought it best to make it back here, rather than struggle to the mainland. I mean, you can't take the chance, can you? But didn't you two see the water coming in? I mean, you must have been several minutes behind me.'

There was an odd, excited tension in his voice as though he was slightly inebriated. Neither Arnold nor Mildred Sauvage-Brown made any reply and the silence that fell became edgy. The man facing them sensed the tension in the hut and he stopped fumbling for his cigarettes. His breath began to rasp in the darkness and he shuffled, turned away, to pull something from his jacket pocket. There was a clicking sound; it came again, and at the third attempt the cigarette-lighter flared, was held out at arm's length. Arnold could see the man's face only dimly, but the flame of the lighter illuminated his own and Miss Sauvage-Brown's.

'Hell's damnation,' the man whispered raggedly. The flame died and there was a long, uncomfortable silence. At last, the man said, 'Mr Landon.'

'That's right.'

'An odd . . . coincidence.'

'I doubt that.'

Mildred Sauvage-Brown cleared her throat. She touched Arnold's shoulder. 'Do . . . do you know this man?'

Arnold nodded in the darkness. 'We've met.'

'Is he the man you've been looking for?'

Arnold's skin prickled. He turned his head, to stare at her in the darkness. He could just make out the line of her sagging features but he could not make out her expression. 'What do you mean? Why do you think I'm looking for someone?'

She was silent for a few moments. She came closer to him, half-whispering, even though the other occupant of the refuge could clearly hear all she said. 'I reached the island before you. I too was up in the graveyard, watching the inn. I saw you come up, and I hid behind the headstones to your left.'

Be careful, Freddie Keeler had warned him. Someone else had been making inquiries about the auction, before him. Arnold now understood why inquiries had been made, and who had made them.

'I was still in the graveyard when you went down. I couldn't follow you, for you'd have seen me, and I just didn't know what to do. Then I saw you walk down the lane after the auctioneer, making your way out towards the headland.'

The man clucked his tongue in the darkness, a nervous reaction based on surprise. But he said nothing, and when Mildred Sauvage-Brown went on her voice had strengthened, courage seeping back into her as she spoke, remembering why she had come here to Lindisfarne.

'I didn't know what to do. I guessed you were looking for the same man I was, but I had no idea how to proceed when you walked down the lane. So I decided to go back to my Land Rover and wait. It was parked on top of the hill, in the village street. It gave me a good view of the village, the castle, and the headland. Then, a few minutes later, I saw the car come down from behind the castle.'

Arnold glanced across to the other occupant of the refuge. He seemed to be standing stiffly in the darkness, hands clenched at his sides, listening intently and almost holding his breath.

'The car came past me,' Mildred Sauvage-Brown grumbled, 'but I didn't know what you were up to, and what was happening. It drove out of the village very fast. I couldn't see who was driving, and although I thought I heard some shouting I couldn't be sure. After a little while I saw you, Mr Landon. You'd been running, but you had begun to stagger. It was then that I guessed what had happened.'

Arnold remembered the vehicle starting up as he climbed the hill in the village, the headlights flashing over him, the acceleration out of the village.

'I just didn't think,' Mildred Sauvage-Brown admitted. 'When I saw you and realized you'd been running after the car, I guessed what had happened and I just drove straight out of the village. After . . . after him.'

She shuddered violently, and Arnold remembered her fear in the car. 'Did you know he was up here?' Arnold asked gently. 'Is that why you wanted to stay in the Land Rover?'

'I couldn't be sure,' she replied. 'There was just the one car left the village before mine — no one else had gone for some time. And when I found that I couldn't go on, with the tide coming in, I realized that he would probably have been stopped as well, with the water coming in so fast. There was the *possibility* that he might have made it to the mainland but I couldn't be sure, and I . . . I was afraid that he might be up here. I didn't *know,* but I didn't want to take the chance.'

'What is this all about?' said the man against the far wall. 'What are you talking about? What have you been doing on Lindisfarne?'

'Looking for you,' Arnold said simply.

The man was silent for a little while. 'I don't understand,' he said finally.

'I think you do.'

'Looking for me? Why should you do that? You know where I live.'

'Yes, I know where you live,' Arnold replied, 'but when I came to Lindisfarne I didn't know you were the person I was seeking.'

'You're talking in riddles.'

'No. And *you* don't believe that either. You know why I've been looking for you.'

The man in the shadows cleared his throat nervously. He rubbed his hands against his thighs as though he were suddenly cold. 'This is stupid. I don't know what you're talking about. I don't know why you're on Lindisfarne, and all this talk about searching for me . . . How can you be sure I'm the person you seek?'

'It's obvious,' Arnold replied. 'Three cars left this island after the tide started to run. The first was driven by a man eager to leave Holy Island after he'd received the report he wanted from the auctioneer acting for him in the sale at the Dog and Whistle. The second vehicle was Miss Sauvage-Brown's Land Rover. I was in the third.'

'Yes, but—'

'You've already told us you were heading for the mainland. There's no one else in this refuge. You have to be the man who drove away from the headland. That means you're the man I'm looking for.'

'Headlands, auctioneers . . . I don't know what you're talking about.' There was a tremor of desperation in the man's voice. 'I've no idea—'

'You know.'

'I swear—'

'You were at the headland, talking to the auctioneer—'

'For what reason, dammit?'

'To discover whether the sale of the Durham missal had been successfully completed!'

There was a long silence, broken only by the rhythm of the rain on the roof of the refuge. The man facing them shifted uncomfortably. At last he said quietly, 'I know nothing about any Durham missal.'

'Don't be a fool,' Arnold said. 'To deny it is a waste of time. It will be no difficult task to trace the auctioneer, eventually. He'll be able to identify you as the person who commissioned him to arrange the sale on Lindisfarne, quietly, among a selected group of persons interested in exclusive, expensive possessions. He'll be able to identify you, and I'll be able to testify you met him at the headland, and found you here later, at the refuge, stranded like us by the rising tide . . .'

'And I,' Mildred Sauvage-Brown added in a harsh whisper, 'will be able to point the finger at the murderer of Sarah Ellis.'

'Murder?'

'You killed her!'

'Listen—'

'You murdered Sarah for that missal!'

'That's crazy!'

* * *

The words had crackled out with a fierce desperation and were followed by a complete silence. Startled by the vehemence in the man's tone, Mildred Sauvage-Brown had stepped back, stumbling against Arnold. Now she stood close to him and she was trembling. Arnold himself felt cold, uncertain what to do or say. They had come this far but the man with them in the refuge had killed once, and the passion in his tone meant that he could be capable of killing again.

'You've got it all wrong,' the man said at last, in a quiet, reasoning tone.

'So tell us.'

The three of them stood still, and the darkness closed around them as the wind rose, beating rain against the roof of the hut in a gentle tattoo. Mildred Sauvage-Brown was shivering. She seemed to have lost all her assertiveness and aggression. She had made the same guess as Arnold, linked the missal to the death of Sarah Ellis, and had started making inquiries about its sale. She had set out, like Arnold, to find out who was selling the missal, but now she had found him her nerve had failed, the anger and desire to revenge Sarah had faded, and she was frightened.

So was Arnold.

'This suggestion,' said the man in front of them, 'it's ridiculous. Even if you can show that I had a missal for sale, it doesn't mean anything. I'll be able to prove to you, and to anyone you tell, that the item I sold was an old family heirloom. I'll be able to demonstrate its provenance—'

'Then why did you find it necessary to sell it secretly, out here on Lindisfarne, away from prying eyes?' Arnold asked.

'I haven't admitted I did sell it yet,' the man replied. 'But if I did . . . there's nothing wrong in dealing with a small group—'

'Unless you stole the missal in the first instance.'

'I didn't steal it!'

'First you say you didn't *sell* it, then you say you didn't *steal* it — you're getting confused,' Arnold said.

'No,' the man said flatly. '*You're* confused. I need say nothing. I need admit nothing. I've done nothing wrong. You have no proof of my involvement in anything, and as far as this Sarah Ellis thing is concerned—'

'What if I were able to prove that the missal you sold belonged to Sarah Ellis?' Arnold asked.

'I haven't *admitted* selling anything yet,' the man said shakily. 'But proof . . . what proof are you talking about?'

'In the morning, when we go to the police, maybe we can put it to the test.'

'Police? Test? What are you talking about?' The man moved restlessly away from the wall, but coming no nearer to them. Nevertheless, Mildred Sauvage-Brown tightened her grip on Arnold's arm.

'It was I who found Sarah Ellis's body at the farm,' Arnold said. 'I was shaken. When I went in, I thought it had been Miss Sauvage-Brown who had been killed. It was only when she arrived with the police that I realized it was Miss Ellis who had been lying there. But the experience coloured my thinking, and my judgment.'

'What's that supposed to mean?'

'I assumed Sarah Ellis had been killed by mistake. I thought the intention might have been to assault and perhaps kill Miss Sauvage-Brown, because of her attempts to prevent the development of Penbrook Farm. As a result, I never thought of other motives, or other intentions.'

Mildred Sauvage-Brown stirred beside him. 'I thought the same thing for a while,' she whispered. 'Oddly, it didn't frighten me. I was enraged. I was determined to find out who had killed poor Sarah.'

'It was some time later,' Arnold went on, 'before I found a sheet of paper at my home. I had been cleaning the place out, cleaning the car, getting my coat repaired — and there was this sheet in the wastepaper bin. I didn't know how it got there, but when I took it to a friend of mine, an antiquarian, he told me it was valuable. Part of a missal printed in Durham. Old, and valuable.'

'So?' The man leaned back against the wall, seeking support. 'What's that got to do with anything here on Lindisfarne?'

'A great deal.' Arnold paused. 'I puzzled for a long time. I could not think how that sheet came into my possession. I went through all my books—'

'I didn't know about all this,' Miss Sauvage-Brown said wonderingly.

'But it wasn't until I saw the photograph in the paper that everything clicked into place.'

'Photograph?' the man said hoarsely.

Arnold nodded. 'The previous occasion when I visited Penbrook Farm a certain . . . altercation ensued. Miss Sauvage-Brown had arrested a surveyor in the barn and was threatening him with a shotgun. The police arrived, and so did reporters and a photographer from the *Journal*. He took a number of shots; one of them was taken when Miss Sauvage-Brown herself was arrested. It was published in the Sunday newspapers. It wasn't a very flattering photograph . . . but in the background was Sarah Ellis. She was clutching something in her hand. Something she always carried with her.'

'All her life she carried it,' Mildred Sauvage-Brown muttered sadly.

'An old missal,' Arnold said.

Silence fell. The man against the wall seemed frozen, incapable of speech, and Arnold waited, the blood beginning to pound in his temples. The man shifted uneasily, and cleared his throat. 'You said something about proof . . .'

'A sheet broke loose from that missal. It came into my possession.' Arnold paused. 'When I heard from my antiquarian friend that a missal — a Durham missal — was up for sale and that it was not in *perfect* condition I put the facts together. Maybe the sheet I held was part of the missal for sale. If it was . . . maybe Sarah Ellis was killed for the missal, *not* in mistake for Mildred Sauvage-Brown . . .'

'I came to the same conclusion myself,' Miss Sauvage-Brown muttered, 'that time I was up at your bungalow. I was standing there, thinking about Sarah, and I saw all those books of yours scattered around in the sitting-room, and I recalled how Sarah had always loved that old missal, took such comfort from it . . . *and it was no longer at the farm*. The police had asked me if anything was missing, but I had been too shaken to think straight, and I'd forgotten, never told them . . .' She stirred, turned her face to stare at Arnold. 'But how did the sheet get into your possession?'

'It took me a long time to work out,' Arnold replied. 'But it happened that day at Penbrook Farm. It was all very confusing. While you were being taken into custody, and everyone was running around the place, I almost forgot about it. The fact is, when you trapped the surveyor in the barn Miss Ellis went running up the lane for help and found me. Her dress was stained and muddy, and she was in such a state she dropped her book. I picked it up, stuffed it in the pocket of my coat while I tried to soothe her and find out what the problem was. I returned it to her when I was leaving Penbrook Farm but one of the pages had worked loose, and remained caught in my pocket. My coat was tom, so I threw it in the back of the car.'

'But you said you found the sheet in the wastepaper basket,' Mildred Sauvage-Brown reminded him.

'That's right. But what happened was that it must have fallen from my coat pocket when the coat was bundled on to the back seat. A few days later I took the car to be washed. I cleaned inside and collected bits and pieces of paper from the car and dumped them in the basket. I didn't notice it until later, when I had started clearing junk out of the house. By then, the chain of events had become blurred . . . I didn't make the connection.'

'All this . . .' began the man in front of Arnold.

'Can be proved,' Arnold interrupted. 'And if you've sold a damaged missal today, a missal with a page missing, and the page I have with a friend in Newcastle turns out to be the page from the missal, you'll have some explaining to do. You'll have to explain how you got your hands on the book, after the page had been lost, and about the same time that Sarah Ellis died.'

'Circumstantial evidence, that's all it would be,' the man demurred, 'merely circumstantial evidence—'

'Sometimes,' Mildred Sauvage-Brown snapped triumphantly, 'it can be very strong, like finding a trout in the milk!'

'What?' the man said in puzzlement but Mildred Sauvage-Brown made no reply.

'The fact is,' Arnold said, 'if the page fits, it brands you as a murderer. You killed Sarah Ellis to steal that missal.'

The man was shaking his head, as though weary of the accusations being made against him. 'You don't understand. You just don't understand any of it. That missal . . . I didn't steal it. The damned thing has been in my family for generations. It was mine. I sold it today, yes, but it was always mine to sell. And that,' Henry Willington added with a sigh, 'is probably the irony of it all.'

4

Arnold stared at the heir to Willington Hall in amazement. He shook his head. 'I don't understand.'

'Why should you?' Henry Willington said wearily. 'The story goes back a long time. Sarah . . . she wasn't called Ellis at all. Her name was really Willington. She was my father's sister. Sarah Ellis was my aunt.'

'Your *aunt?*' Mildred Sauvage-Brown bristled. '*Willington?* That's not possible! She . . .' Her grip slackened on Arnold's arm and she stood up straighter. She peered at Henry Willington across the dark-shadowed room. 'And yet . . . she was odd about names. I told you, Mr Landon, that time I came to your bungalow. She'd made a will years ago, but the name she used then was *Willis*. When I met her she called herself *Ellis*.'

'But originally she was called Willington, believe me,' Henry Willington asserted. 'But I can understand her not wanting to use it. She hated it; hated the family—'

'But how long have you known she was living at Penbrook Farm?' Arnold asked.

'I didn't know at all — neither did my father. I'd never even seen her — I thought she was probably dead, and my father certainly thought so. It was quite a shock that Sunday morning, when he saw her photograph in the newspaper.' Henry Willington was silent for a little while. 'The shock, and the anger it generated brought on his stroke, I think. He died the same day.'

'Anger?' Mildred Sauvage-Brown queried.

'I told you,' Henry Willington said in a tired voice. 'It all goes back a long, long time. My father was an autocratic bastard when he wanted to be. And he caused her trouble, when she was about twenty or so.'

'What sort of trouble?' Arnold asked.

'Oh, I don't really know the details of it. And I only heard my father's side of it, and he'd have been biased, of course. In a nutshell, it seems that his young sister Sarah conceived an affection for one of the local lads around Willington Hall. Sarah fell in love, head over heels, but my father — her brother — wasn't pleased. I understand he felt she was lowering herself, going below her station in life. He could be incredibly Victorian at times.'

'So what happened?'

'Not sure, exactly. He busted it up, that's for certain. How, I don't know, but he waded in, interfered, made sure that Sarah and this friend of hers would never get together. But the result couldn't have been what my father expected.'

'How do you mean?' Mildred Sauvage-Brown asked.

'She didn't take it lying down, did young Sarah. She up and left Willington Hall and my father never saw her again. He made some inquiries, and discovered she had gone to the Continent under an assumed name. He did trace her a couple of times, but then she disappeared for good and he gave up. She had money of her own, that had come to her from her mother's side of the family, and she was independent, she could afford to live well enough all those years. He didn't care, anyway. There was just one thing that rankled — it was the reason why he had tried to find her at all.'

'Reason?' Arnold asked.

Henry Willington was silent for a while. He seemed to be thinking, dredging up the past and inspecting it, not liking, perhaps, what he saw, of his father, his aunt and himself. 'Well,' he said, 'when she left, she didn't go empty-handed.'

'How do you mean?'

'She hated my father; hated him for what he had done to her life, in destroying her chance of happiness with the man she had fallen for. She clearly decided to leave Willington Hall and never return, and she took all her personal possessions—'

'Including love-letters,' Mildred Sauvage-Brown said in a sad tight voice. 'Love-letters she kept for half a century.'

'—but she also wanted to get her revenge on her brother. So she took something of his. Something he valued highly. An item he cherished, even though he might have had to sell it to support the Hall in later years. She took it to hurt him as much as she could—'

'Good for her,' Mildred Sauvage-Brown muttered.

'The missal,' Arnold said quietly.

'That's right. It had been willed to my father. It was a prized possession. Sarah's taking it with her made him mad as hell. It's why he pursued her to the Continent. It's why she changed her name.'

'And it must have given her great satisfaction to have returned, years later, to live in the same county as her brother, with the missal, knowing he would always bleed over its loss,' Mildred Sauvage-Brown said. 'Good for you, Sarah!'

'So you'll understand,' Henry Willington said in a flat voice, 'just how great a shock it was for my father when he saw the photograph. He recognized her. *My God*, he said, *that's Sarah. And she's got the missal with her still!*' Henry Willington paused. 'He was apoplectic with rage. He started to cough. Then he had a stroke. I called the doctor, but he wasn't long in dying.'

'Sarah obtained her revenge at the end,' Mildred Sauvage-Brown said.

'And you got Willington Hall,' Arnold said to Henry Willington.

The man shuffled. He stepped forward, shaking his head. 'It wasn't intentional . . . I hadn't planned it that way . . . But when my father died, imagine the position! For years

I'd tried to persuade him to let me have the managing of the estate. Instead of that, he persisted in his hare-brained schemes, dragging the estate down. And when he died, and I received control and ownership of the Hall, what was left for me? A decaying property, worn-out farms, a situation that was all but beyond redemption. He'd left me nothing! Like his own father before him, he'd bled the estate, in his own way.'

'But there was the photograph,' Arnold said, the hairs prickling on the back of his neck as he saw the inexorable logic of the thoughts that would have gone through Henry Willington's mind.

'That's right. The photograph. It had killed my father – in a sense it had given me Willington Hall. But it also gave me something else. A lifeline. A chance to save the estate. That missal didn't belong to my aunt Sarah. It was my father's. And on his death, it belonged to me. And it could help me bring Willington Hall back into shape! If I could retrieve it, sell it, I could use the money to rejuvenate Willington!'

'So you went to Penbrook Farm?' Mildred SauvageBrown asked. 'You went there that day, when I hadn't returned from Morpeth?'

'Her address was there in the news item. I went there,' Henry Willington said, his voice faltering slightly, 'but nothing went the way I'd planned. I'd hoped to persuade her, thought that she'd be pleased to meet her nephew after all these years, and I hoped we could come to some kind of accommodation . . . But it wasn't like that.'

'Sarah could be a very determined lady,' Mildred Sauvage-Brown said sadly.

'When I told her who I was she told me she had always hated my father, and had certainly taken the missal to revenge herself on him, but now she regarded it as her own. It never left her possession; it was as though it was a reminder of the man she had lost as a young woman, and nothing would now induce her to part with it. She would never give it to me. Perhaps when she died . . .'

'You tried to take it from her,' Arnold said flatly.

'But it was mine! And I could use it to save the Hall!' The rain increased, the pattering sound turning to a drumming on the wooden roof of the refuge. 'I went there, introduced myself and tried to explain. She was unreasonable; she simply wouldn't listen, or even try to understand! All right, maybe we were two of a kind apart from the blood link — I with my obsession, she with hers. But what use was the missal to her? What good was it doing?'

'She cherished it,' Mildred Sauvage-Brown said fiercely.

'But its sale could make an immense difference to the future of Willington Hall!' Henry Willington glared at her for several seconds, before adding angrily, 'And it was mine after all. *Legally*, it was mine!'

'So what happened?' Arnold asked.

'She refused to give it to me. She was holding it, clutching it to her. I can't be sure what happened then, really. I suppose I lost control . . . the frustrations of all the years with my father blocking every attempt to bring order to the chaos . . . and now this old woman insisting on clinging to something that didn't belong to her when the reason for her revenge was already dead . . .'

'You tried to take it from her.'

'She was surprisingly strong,' Henry Willington said. 'Determined. She held on . . . I was afraid the thing would get damaged . . . I didn't hit her, or anything like that. I got hold of the missal, I swung her away from me, and suddenly, when she lost her grip, the determination seemed to disappear and she was light as a bird . . . She crashed against the wall. She didn't make a sound after that, and I saw the blood, and I didn't know what to do. I pulled her into the corner . . .'

His breathing was laboured in the silence of the room. Above them the rain drummed with increasing intensity and in the distance there was the low growl of thunder. 'I was frightened,' Willington went on quietly. 'I was afraid I might be seen leaving the farm entrance so I smashed the light-bulbs . . . I imagine that will be seen as evidence of deliberation . . . but it wasn't like that.'

He moved across to the window and stared out into the blackness the rain streaming down the glass.

Beside Arnold, Mildred Sauvage-Brown shifted uneasily. 'What now?' she asked.

Arnold felt wet and cold and despondent. The fear that had touched him, the prickling at the back of his neck when he had heard Henry Willington's voice above them on the ladder, all that had gone. Misery gripped him and he wished fervently he had not come to Lindisfarne and never heard of Penbrook Farm, but was lying warm in his bed at Morpeth.

'What do we do now?' Mildred Sauvage-Brown insisted.

'We wait,' Arnold replied. 'We wait for morning.'

5

'Early retirement?' Arnold repeated in astonishment.

The Chief Executive grimaced, exposing his perfectly aligned teeth in an unconscious attempt to demonstrate their perfection. 'That's right. We couldn't follow up suggestions of redundancy for the Senior Planning Officer, because clearly we'll need to fill the post. So I had a chat with him, and we decided upon a . . . er . . . strategy.'

'But he's only in his early fifties,' Arnold protested.

'Age, in these circumstances, is irrelevant.'

'Circumstances?'

The Chief Executive thought for a moment, considering matters of great portent, then reluctantly waved Arnold to a chair. It was leather, and deeply comfortable: only in the office of the Chief Executive were such chairs to be found.

The Chief Executive grimaced again, raised his eyes to the ceiling, steepled his fingers and decided. 'In part, Mr Landon, you are responsible.'

'For the Senior Planning Officer's decision?'

'One might say so.'

'How?'

'I run a pretty tight ship, Mr Landon. I was not in command here when you were employed in this department so you won't have had occasion to come under my controls. But my petty officers, they tell me things, keep me informed.'

Arnold had heard about the Chief Executive's 'controls'. One of them was nicknamed 'Sniveller' Samson. A clerk in the legal section, he had the ear of the Chief Executive, and used it.

'It followed that when information reached me concerning your visits to my department I arranged to have a few questions asked. Certain issues then came to light.'

'Issues?'

'Precisely. I was told you'd been asking questions, looking at files . . . on certain matters and about certain people.'

'Like Councillor Minford.'

'And Mrs Minford, and her firm of building contractors.' The Chief Executive sighed. 'Command can be a lonely, and quite precarious business, Mr Landon. To protect my own frigate I found it necessary to send out my own reconnaissance units. After all, if there had been any corruption, and I hadn't investigated it . . .'

'And *has* there been?'

'I didn't say that.'

'But the Senior Planning Officer—'

'Is retiring early,' the Chief Executive interrupted, 'and at his own request. He agrees that he . . . ah . . . became rather too closely involved with certain business interests. Early retirement would seem to be the most appropriate solution.'

'What about the business interests you mention? I take it you're talking about Wilson and Livingstone?'

The Chief Executive's glance came down from the ceiling in irritation. 'I mentioned no names. Suffice it to say that I have had a discreet word with the Leader of the Council and certain suggestions have been made in certain quarters. Thereafter, it's nothing to do with me. I have done my duty. Beyond that, it's a matter for your own department. Planning, after all, does lie there. I merely command the whole ship. Which brings me to the reason for my calling you here. Your future . . .'

'*I* hadn't contemplated early retirement, Chief Executive—'

'No, no,' the Chief Executive said hastily, 'I wasn't about to discuss that kind of proposal with you. Not at all. I mean, if you and the Senior Planning Officer were to retire from the department at the same time the press would smell a witch-hunt and who knows what wild allegations might be made about council and business activities!'

'Then—'

'We shall have to bring in someone new, of course, to succeed the Senior Planning Officer. It's clear we cannot offer the post to you, for you have no qualifications to support your application, and there are certain other matters . . .'

'I've no wish to apply,' Arnold said. 'I'm quite happy where I am.'

'I'm pleased to hear that,' the Chief Executive murmured unconvincingly. 'So we'll advertise; and a new head of the department will be appointed. Which brings me to the other matters. They can be summed up in one word, Mr Landon. Attitude.'

'Chief Executive?'

'*Attitude*. I'm sure you do good work, in the planning department. But this . . . leaning towards the extraordinary, this . . . peculiarity of interest you have, can you promise me it will become somewhat more . . . muted in future? Concentrate on your job, Mr Landon, please do.'

'I'm not conscious that my interests interfere with my work, Chief Executive, but I take your words in the spirit they are meant.'

'That's good,' the Chief Executive said, hooding his eyes in satisfaction. 'Rather more *muted*, that's the answer.'

As he left the room, Arnold was almost certain he heard the Chief Executive add under his breath, 'And then maybe we'll have rather fewer corpses around the place . . .'

* * *

Two days after the advertisement for the Senior Planning Officer's successor was placed, Mildred Sauvage-Brown came to see Arnold. She made no appointment, but simply barged unannounced into his room. Clearly, she considered that as a public servant he had no right to expect courtesies from members of the public.

'It's a cover-up,' she announced, 'and I won't stand for it.'

'What's a cover-up?'

'Minford. Wilson. Livingstone.'

Patiently, Arnold said, 'But it's what you've been campaigning for! The public inquiry has been cancelled. The development application for Penbrook Farm has been withdrawn. The plans for the Minford Twilight Home have now been changed: the home will be built on the outskirts of Morpeth, and Minford's name will not be associated with it. Haven't you won everything you've been fighting for?'

'As far as all *that* is concerned,' she said breathlessly, 'of course! But it's the way it's been done that I simply can't countenance. No scandal has been uncovered; no corruption unearthed! You know as well as I do that my allegations about Wilson and Livingstone and Minford and all the chicanery of the contracts behind the Penbrook Farm were true.'

'But difficult, if not impossible, to prove.'

'And the solution is quietly to advise those bastards to withdraw, there's no mud-slinging, and it's all dealt with behind closed doors? That's not my way, Mr Landon!'

'It's the way of politics, Miss Sauvage-Brown.'

'Humph.'

'You've got your way. And you live to fight another day.'

'Humph.' Some of the anger died in her eyes and she sat down, uninvited, a dumpy, vaguely unhappy middle-aged woman in a hacking jacket and tweed skirt. 'Sarah didn't live to fight any more battles.'

Arnold made no reply. There seemed nothing to say.

'Henry Willington's up for trial soon,' she said. 'What do you think he'll get?'

'I think he'll be found guilty of manslaughter. The term of imprisonment . . .' Arnold shrugged.

'What about the missal?'

'It was legally his. There's no question of confiscation on the grounds of a killer not being allowed to profit from his crime.'

'But what'll happen to the money he got from the sale?'

'Most of it will go to pay off accumulated debts on Willington Hall. The rest will be waiting for him, I imagine, when he gets out of jail. I'm not sure he'll enjoy it much.'

'Perhaps not.' Mildred Sauvage-Brown frowned. 'Poor Sarah . . . it was all so unnecessary.' She rose abruptly. 'But I have the farm and I shall run it as Sarah and I had decided. I shall save that mediaeval woodland, and the tiles on the pigsty . . .' She paused, jutted out her lower lip in thought, looked back reluctantly. Her brow was thunderous with uncertainty and her tone was uneasy. 'I suppose I ought to thank you, Mr Landon.'

Equally uneasy, Arnold replied, 'It's not necessary.'

'You *did* help, in your way.'

'I was doing my job.'

'Yes . . . But perhaps I was a bit . . . over the top, accusing you at the inquiry of being a traitor.'

'It's all over and done with, Miss Sauvage-Brown.'

'Even so . . .' Mildred Sauvage-Brown shuffled in discomfort. She was not used to making apologies and she was equally nervous about developing relationships. 'Fact is, with your job and my . . . interests, our paths are likely to cross from time to time.'

Arnold hoped not.

'There's the Amble thing, for instance,' she went on. 'The marina. Quite wrong. No one wants it.'

'You'll have no status at that inquiry, Miss Sauvage-Brown,' Arnold said, alarmed.

'No, but I'll have to speak out! I mean, there must be some sort of fiddle going on there. Public money involved. Corruption!'

'Miss Sauvage-Brown—'

She was walking out into the corridor. Over her shoulder, reluctantly, she was muttering, 'If I do get a bit . . . well . . . you know, excited, and say things that are a bit . . . extreme, I hope you won't take offence. It won't be that I don't respect your point of view . . . or your professionalism.'

He followed her into the corridor. She was stepping into the lift. Her face was faintly flushed as she looked at him, the doors closing upon her. 'I just hope you won't take it personally,' she said.

The doors sighed and she was gone. There were workmen in the corridor, taking away the coffee machine. When it had 'leaned' upon the office cleaner it probably hadn't intended the unfortunate lady to take it personally either, Arnold thought gloomily.

He hoped the successor to the Senior Planning Officer would be appointed before the Amble inquiry started. He went back to his office and made himself an illegal, but infinitely superior, cup of coffee.

At the weekend he'd drive out to the Nine Nicks of Thirlwall. There were always compensations.

THE END

ALSO BY ROY LEWIS

ERIC WARD MYSTERIES

Book 1: THE SEDLEIGH HALL MURDER
Book 2: THE FARMING MURDER
Book 3: THE QUAYSIDE MURDER
Book 4: THE DIAMOND MURDER
Book 5: THE GEORDIE MURDER
Book 6: THE SHIPPING MURDER
Book 7: THE CITY OF LONDON MURDER
Book 8: THE APARTMENT MURDER
Book 9: THE SPANISH VILLA MURDER
Book 10: THE MARRIAGE MURDER
Book 11: THE WASTEFUL MURDER
Book 12: THE PHANTOM MURDER
Book 13: THE SLAUGHTERHOUSE MURDER
Book 14: THE TATTOO MURDER
Book 15: THE FOOTBALL MURDER
Book 16: THE TUTANKHAMUN MURDER
Book 17: THE ZODIAC MURDER

INSPECTOR JOHN CROW

Book 1: A LOVER TOO MANY
Book 2: ERROR OF JUDGMENT
Book 3: THE WOODS MURDER
Book 4: MURDER FOR MONEY
Book 5: MURDER IN THE MINE
Book 6: A COTSWOLDS MURDER
Book 7: A FOX HUNTING MURDER
Book 8: A DARTMOOR MURDER

ARNOLD LANDON MYSTERIES

Book 1: MURDER IN THE BARN
Book 2: MURDER IN THE MANOR
Book 3: MURDER IN THE FARMHOUSE

Thank you for reading this book.

If you enjoyed it please leave feedback on Amazon or Goodreads, and if there is anything we missed or you have a question about, then please get in touch. We appreciate you choosing our book.

Founded in 2014 in Shoreditch, London, we at Joffe Books pride ourselves on our history of innovative publishing. We were thrilled to be shortlisted for Independent Publisher of the Year at the British Book Awards.

www.joffebooks.com

We're very grateful to eagle-eyed readers who take the time to contact us. Please send any errors you find to corrections@joffebooks.com. We'll get them fixed ASAP.

Printed in Great Britain
by Amazon

83401422R00123